Shallow Water Romance

A Story of Forbidden Love and Adventure

by

Anna Leigh

A Sandy Bay Romance

Dedication

For Debbie Crews – An Incredible and Fascinating woman.
Intelligent, Strong and Beautiful. Consummate professional, leader and manager. An Inspiration.
And Friend
May all your days be filled with happiness and success.

PMΓ

Anna Leigh

ACKNOWLEDGMENTS

No book can be completed without the help of many others, usually too numerous to mention all by name. Here are a few, and forgive me if I have excluded someone – I would write someone important, but you are all important to me.

First, my family without who's encouragement this would have not been completed. Especially my mom, who always believed. Then, to the group of reviewers who provide valuable insight and impetus for changing this work in ways to make it better, and to all those others for helping me to accomplish my goals – my readers who have made this effort a joy, especially Becky, Laura, Sally, Kasima, and Bo for their assistance and support.

Finally, my gratitude and debt to the editor of this work, Jessica Snyder, who not only offered great insights and ideas to make this a better work, but also provided encouragement and praise.

Cover by Saveht
at 99designs

There are only four questions of value in life...
What is sacred?
Of what is the spirit made?
What is worth living for?
What is worth dying for?
The answer to each is same. Only love.

Johnny Depp
Don Juan DeMarco

They say that bears
Have love affairs
And even camels
We're merely mammals
Let's misbehave.

Let's Misbehave
Cole Porter

Where we start out in the world does not
Determine where we end up.

One

Dee Cruise was driving up the coast. She had the road to herself. The ocean was to her left, deep blue in the rays of the morning sun. Her window was down and the late spring breeze felt cool on her face. It tousled her hair. How different California was from the east coast! She smiled at her good fortune to have gotten this assignment, but her happiness was tempered knowing that her good fortune was the result, at least in part, of someone else's misfortune.

That song began playing again on the radio. She loved that song, but they never announced what it actually was. How was she going to download it if she didn't know the name? By the time she got to work, she knew she'd forget to look up the station's playlist to see what it was. She'd asked her smart phone what it was, but all she got back was nonsense.

"What is the title of the song that is playing?"

"I'm sorry, what long title did you want?"

"No! Not long title! Song title!"

"What song did you want the title for?"

"The song that's playing now."

"I'm sorry. Would you like another song? What song title would you like to hear?"

It would have gone on longer, but the song ended. She wondered if the designers of the so-called smart phones had designed in a little stupidity, or mischievousness. She had gotten so frustrated at times that she'd once asked if the phone would like to take a trip to the shooting range. "Why would we go the shooting range?" it asked. "It will be a surprise," she'd answered with a smile.

She looked at her watch. It was 7:35. She could stop for a cup of coffee – takeout – and still be at her new station on time.

The road became rougher, and the front of her car dipped. What was that?

"Dammit!" The vehicle pulled to one side and she knew it was the left front tire.

She edged the car off the asphalt and onto the shoulder. Gravel crunched beneath the tires as the car rolled to a stop on its own. She knew better than to apply the brakes, especially if the flat was a front tire.

She got out of the car and looked. Sure enough, left front. "Dammit!"

There went the coffee. She'd be lucky to get to the station on time. The car was new – well, almost new, and she'd never changed a tire on this one. It had been many years since she'd changed a tire at all.

She looked around. The lovely solitary drive had changed to stuck alone on a road. She slid back into the driver's seat and opened the glove compartment. After a minute, she located the manual and paged through it to find the procedure for changing the tire – most importantly, the lift point for the jack. Her father had stressed how important putting the jack in the right place was. Well, that was to her brother, not to her. But she'd overheard. Even as he'd said, "This is man's work; not women's work." Good old dad. He believed in strict gender roles, and was always finding a way to make her feel she should just stay in the kitchen.

She found the page and scanned the procedure. She was happy there were plenty of pictures. She hated pure descriptions. She'd put together a bookcase from instructions that had no pictures. *'Slide shelf D between uprights A and B. Use dowel L to fasten the center-most blah, blah, blah.'* By the time she was done with that bookcase she was completely frustrated and had a sculpture that even Picasso would have trouble loving.

She got out to the car and headed for the back, smiling as she thought about when she'd bought a new, already assembled bookcase, then consigned the one she'd put together to her fireplace.

She raised the hatch back, pulled out the floor liner, and with some difficulty, she removed the spare and the jack. She wheeled the tire to the driver-side door and rested it there. She proceeded to position the jack and raise the car until the deflated tire was off the ground. Her arm was tired. She rubbed it with her left hand. She put the lug wrench on the first lug and tried to turn it. The whole wheel turned. She tried again, with the same result. She tried bracing her foot against the tire, but again, the tire turned before the lug's hold would break. She deflated.

She could call a garage – or the auto club for assistance, but then she'd be just another helpless woman who couldn't change a tire. Who was she kidding? She *was* that helpless woman who couldn't change a tire.

There was the sound of an approaching vehicle. An old but polished red pickup truck pulled off the road and behind her car. No need to worry. Or was there? The lonely road was lonelier, despite – maybe because of – the presence of one other vehicle. How many bad endings had started out with, 'Her car broke down on a lonely road?'

Something inside her was twisting and turning. Oh, good. She could see the headline now. *Woman abducted, raped and murdered after car breaks down on coast road.* She shook her head, but the thoughts and feeling didn't disappear completely. The truck stopped and the door opened. She saw faded jeans and cowboy boots, under the door. Her mouth was dry and her pulse quickened. When a man stepped out from behind the door, she saw he was wearing a white t-shirt, tucked into his jeans. His hair was a light brown, and he was tan. Tan and muscular. Not overbuilt – athletic, and definitely in shape. But even nice-looking guys could be dangerous.

"May I give you a hand, ma'am?"

"I'm doing okay. It'll just take me a few minutes and I'll have this changed." The dryness was still in her mouth. Her heartbeat was fast and strong. Her hand tightened around the tire iron. Just in case.

"I thought you might want some assistance."

"Is it because men seem to think that women are helpless and can't change a tire? I really don't need any help." *And, I'm not about to hand over my only weapon to a complete stranger.*

"Yes, ma'am, I'm sure. The reason I asked was you seem to be dressed for work — and not dirty work, and I'm dressed for — well, pretty much for changing tires. But, if you'd rather —"

"Yes, thank you. Thank you for stopping. I didn't mean to sound —"

"No ma'am. No problem. I just thought I'd offer." He walked back to his truck, got in and started it. He pulled back onto the road and stopped parallel to where she was. "Just a suggestion, ma'am, but if you want to loosen those lugs, you might lower the vehicle until the tire is on the ground. That'll keep the wheel from spinning while you loosen them. After that, you can raise the car and remove them, change the tire and put the lug nuts back in place. Don't forget to tighten the them all the way with the tire resting on the ground. Have a good day, ma'am." And he was gone.

"Son of a — ," but she stopped herself there. She proceeded to do as he'd said, the process working perfectly. Her father had chased her off when he'd spotted her listening in to his conversation with her brother, so she hadn't learned the trick with the tire. And, if she had to be truthful, she'd only seen a tire changed after that. She hadn't actually done it herself. She had some trouble getting the tire into the well in the back, but if she hurried, she could still get to work on time – if there weren't any police giving tickets this morning.

Twenty minutes later, she pulled into her parking spot – a few minutes late. She'd have to wipe some of the dirt from her uniform. She'd been careful, but you can only be so careful when changing a tire. She frowned. Not the first impression she wanted to make.

She left her vehicle and walked to the front, she assumed it was the front, of the building. The main station building appeared to be an old red brick airplane hangar. It was the size of a high school gymnasium and there was a large open door facing the ocean. A concrete ramp led from the front of the building into the water. Inside the open area were a number of watercraft, sitting on a concrete floor, some in various stages of disassembly and repair. Along the insides of the building were offices. Office fronts were dark wood from the floor to about three feet and glass from there to the ceiling. She found her office, and as she tried to wipe the dirt from her uniform, the administrative assistant came in – Annie. Annie Duncan. She'd talked with her frequently on the phone after she'd gotten her orders. Dee considered her a friend already.

"Good morning, lieutenant. Can I help you?" Annie was petite, blond hair and pale. She was wearing a blue polka dot shirt waist dress and matching blue block heels.

"Um, no. Thank you. Flat tire on the way to work." Dee held out her hand, "I'm very glad to finally meet you."

"I'm glad to meet you, too. Can I get you some coffee?"

"Yes. Please. I missed out on getting a cup because of the tire. A guy stopped. Said he wanted to help, but you never know. I thought I might be abducted – or worse. You see it on TV all the time." She paused, took a deep breath and let it out. "What's on the agenda? I'm probably behind, but I'll try to make it up."

"Yes. I'll get your coffee. The senior NCO – Chief Jackson, is first on the agenda. He's been waiting for you to arrive. I'll call him."

"Thank you." He could wait an additional minute or two. She was the new Officer in Charge and she needed another few moments to herself.

Annie returned with the coffee on a tray. She opened the door by butting into it backwards, set the tray on the desk, and plopped into the chair across from Dee. She crossed her legs and sat semi-reclined. "If you have a minute."

"Of course," she said glancing furtively at the clock.

"It's nice to have a woman here."

"What? There are women here, aren't there?"

"Yes. Well, and don't get me wrong, but the young enlisted women and I don't have a lot in common. I'm not into sleezy bar hopping. I'm not being snobbish, but I'm hoping maybe you and I –"

"Well, why don't we chat a little later – after I see the – chief." Was that true? Were there no other women to make friends with? Well, none her age?

"Great. Thank you. Don't panic, it's just nice to think there is someone here I can relate to." Annie smiled, got up and left.

Dee sat behind her desk and waited for the chief. He arrived five minutes later. She was sipping her coffee and about to let him know she would not tolerate being kept waiting, but when she looked up, there was the tan, good-looking man with the light brown hair who had stopped to help her. Now, he was in short-sleeved summer uniform with a chest full of ribbons.

"Maritime Law Enforcement Specialist Chief Scott Jackson reporting as ordered, ma'am."

She almost spilled the coffee into her lap. *Oh, crap!*

Two

Dee walked down the inside of the hangar and knocked on the door of Annie Duncan's small office. She judged the room to be about ten by fifteen or so. The right wall was covered by filing cabinets. The back wall had bulletins, policies, and orders posted under the pictures of the President, the Secretary of Homeland Security, the Commandant of the Coast Guard, and the Commander of the Eleventh District. The left wall had a small table with a one-cup hot beverage maker and a compact refrigerator.

Annie motioned for her to enter. "No need to knock. Nothing ever happens in here that you would interrupt. Sadly. Have a seat."

"Thank you." Dee plopped deflated into the wood arm chair.

"That was a pretty short meeting. I make it five minutes." She was flipping a pencil up and down between two fingers.

"More like two. Turns out the guy who I thought might rape and kidnap me is the highly decorated chief petty officer here."

Annie snickered until she snorted. The pencil stopped moving. "Sorry."

"Yeah, well, I guess it would be funny to everyone else." Dee crossed her legs and turned slightly in the chair.

"Did he, um, mention anything about your earlier meeting?" She stifled a laugh.

"He said he was glad I didn't have any trouble changing the tire. I felt like such an idiot. So, I introduced myself and apologized for being such a —"

"Independent woman?"

Dee gave her a faux peeved look. "You're having fun with this, aren't you? Yes. I said I was delayed by the flat, and needed to take care of a few things and we could meet again — maybe this afternoon. I just wanted to introduce myself and meet him."

"Which you actually did before." Annie dropped the pencil on the desk.

"You're not helping. You know, I really, really wanted this assignment to go well. This isn't the start I'd hoped for. I didn't exactly make the impression I wanted."

"Chief Jackson isn't the kind of man who will take this seriously. Don't worry."

"I didn't want to start out on his bad side." she said sitting up.

"You don't have to worry about that," Annie said. "But you need to know that Chief Jackson keeps this place running on an even keel. OICs come and go, but since he arrived here, things have worked. It wouldn't do to antagonize him unduly."

"But I'm the one in charge. The officer in charge."

"Well, yes and no. You can give the orders, but there are a thousand details you don't know. A thousand things he's learned over his career. What a lot of young officers don't understand is the chief can make or break them," Annie finished and leaned back in her chair.

"On purpose? Like sabotage?!"

"No. It's just that he can make things go well – sometimes by doing the little extras and heading off any problems – or not so well by following the OICs orders to the letter."

Like the little trick with the lug nuts when changing a tire. "So, what's the best way to stay on his good side?"

"Not so hard. His priorities are doing the job – and doing it right, protecting the service, and helping the enlisted move their careers forward."

"And how does he get along with the enlisted?"

"Most of them would kill for him. Almost literally."

"Men and women?" Dee asked.

"Yes. Both. He gets the best out of them – mostly by example, then challenging them."

"I hate to, but I have to ask." Dee leaned forward. "Any rumors or more about him and the enlisted women?"

"No. None. Not that some of them wouldn't like there to be – something, that is. Not that I wouldn't like to have him throw a little amorous intent my way. If you haven't noticed, he's one nice slice of prime beef."

"Okay. Wait." Dee frowned slightly. "Let's not compare him to a piece of meat."

"Prime," said Annie, with a smile and a twinkle in her eye.

"Still. Even if I were interested, there are regulations. And, my career is the most important thing right now."

"Good." Annie's smile and twinkle faded slightly. "One less in the competition. Not that anyone is going to win. Nice to think about, though. And, that successful career won't keep you warm on a cold night."

"I'll turn up the heat."

"You don't understand."

"I do. I'm just focused."

"You'll end up being a crazy cat woman." Annie leaned forward and her voice dropped to a whisper. "Anyway, he was married once. Something happened. Fast. He stayed in one of the duty rooms for a week or so, until he got an apartment. Nice place, by the way – his apartment – he has parties for the station a couple of times a year. I get to go, too. If you get to go, you'll be the first OIC invited. Tough for an officer to get an invite. Anyway, the soon-to-be-ex called a couple of times way back when. Wouldn't talk to her. Shouldn't tell you this, but I know she isn't getting any of his money. So, she must have done something terrible and got caught."

"We're off the subject. What might I want to do – sort of first thing? Other than review personnel records."

"Kill joy." Annie sat back. "Do a plant property inventory. That will tell you whether we have all the big-ticket items you signed for when you took over. Lieutenant Commander Biggs did one when he left, but it's good business to double check. He coulda lied. You'd be stuck. Then, have the chief show you all the physical plant – what needs to be fixed, upgraded. That ought to take a week or so. Make you look like you know what you're doing. We can figure out more later."

"Sounds like you, not the chief, run the place."

"This is easy stuff. Anybody would know. The chief knows all the ins and outs."

"Okay. Thank you. Could you get me the personnel files?"

"Sure. Just don't leave them out for anybody to see." Annie had become the professional.

Three

Chief Scott Jackson entered his small office and plopped into the chair at his desk. He rotated his head to work out the tightness in his muscles.

"Not much of a meeting," came a voice from behind him.

He turned to see First Class Petty Officer Vincent Ayala sitting on the worn leather couch that was against the wall behind him.

"Yeah, well, I didn't really expect it to be. I was right. That was her fixing the flat on the road in."

"The new L T?" He pronounced it as El Tee.

"Yeah. She came mildly unglued when I asked her if she needed help. One of those 'I can do anything you can do' types. May not bode well for life here at our little station."

"I don't know. We need to give her a chance. Besides, if she'd known who you are her response might have been different."

"Yeah, well, we'll see. If a brand-new lieutenant – who's spent most of her short career at a big house shuffling papers – thinks she know everything about running a small operational station, it's going to be a long tour."

"You're just bitter."

Scott shot him a glance. "I'm not bitter."

Ayala held his eyes, not giving in to Scott's challenge. "One woman has colored your outlook on life. You're bitter and you will be until you get past believing that all women are the same."

Scott looked away. "I'm fine. And it doesn't have anything to do with her being a woman. We've got a newbie who has almost no operational experience. Male or female, I'd like to know the station is in safe hands."

"Well, tell yourself whatever you need to. I wanted to know how it went. I guess I'll do the preventive maintenance on the number two boat." He got off the couch and sauntered out the door.

Scott sat back in his chair. Bullshit. It doesn't have anything to do with – with her. My personal life and professional lives are separate. Anyway, better get to it. Annie probably tell her to do a plant property and facilities inspection. He went to a filing cabinet and pulled out paperwork on the last inspections he did a few months ago.

Four

Dee closed the personnel folder and placed it on the mahogany desk in front of her. To her left was a head – or bathroom – complete with shower, and a small room adjacent with a single bed, or rack, dresser, nightstand and closet – in case she decided, or needed, to spend the night. To her right, bookcases, only partially filled. Behind her a wall for her plaques and pictures. In front of her, like Annie's office, the wall was wood from the floor to about three feet; glass from there to the ceiling.

The building and office were old. It didn't matter. The furnishings were old and worn. It didn't matter, either. It was what she saw on the door that gave her a warm, tingly feeling.

United States Coast Guard Station
Sandy Bay
Lieutenant Dee M. Cruise, USCG
Officer in Charge

Officer in Charge. She was on her way. Later, she might be an executive officer, XO, and finally commanding officer, or CO. It wouldn't be easy, there would be a lot of hard work, but she was plotting her path. This assignment was a stepping stone. She would have to do well here. But career was everything, and she was going to give it her all. She had a warm glow inside her.

Annie stuck her head in the door without knocking. "Brass! Heads up."

The warm glow was replaced by mild anxiety. There was a fluttering in her stomach. *What is "the brass" doing here?* She looked quickly around the office to see if anything was out of place and decided to straighten the folder on her desk. After one week, there wasn't enough in her office yet to be out of place. She looked at the full-length mirror to make sure her uniform was perfect.

A Coast Guard captain appeared outside the glass wall. Just before entering the office, he paused and looked around the large open area in the center of the building where the small watercraft were stored and maintained. He didn't bother to knock, but opened the door and stepped into the office before closing the door behind him.

Dee came to attention behind her desk. "Good morning, Sir. How may I help you?" She read his name tag, but already knew who he was, Frank Trahir, her superior officer. The letter appointing her had indicated she would report to him.

He didn't answer right away. Instead, he looked casually around the office. As the seconds passed, a bird in her stomach fluttered about. Then, there were more, it seemed. She wasn't sure she could stand still. The officer who could make or break her career was essentially ignoring her. *What's he doing? Why is ignoring me?* He ran his finger across a cabinet and looked at it, as if formally inspecting the office. *Oh, god! I hope it's clean.*

"Could I get you something to drink, Captain?"

It took a moment for him to answer. Without looking at her. "Uh, yes. Coffee. One cream. One sugar."

She went to a cabinet where she'd placed a single-cup coffee maker she'd purchased the day before. With a trembling hand, she dropped a k-cup into the machine and placed a mug under the spigot. When she turned, she saw the captain's eyes on her. He said nothing, and anxiety turned to unease. His manner was stern. *What is he doing? And why? Is this an attempt to fluster me, or have I done something already to get myself into trouble?*

The coffee finished brewing. Dee placed one packet of sugar into the coffee and added half and half from a small refrigerator, silently thanking herself for stopping to get dairy and avoiding having to use powdered artificial creamer.

Captain Trahir stepped into the small bunk room and looked around. He opened the closet and moved uniforms she'd placed there aside. Then, he stepped into the head, looked around, opened the mirrored medicine cabinet and looked in there. *Hey, those are MY things.* Although her spaces were subject to routine inspection, she felt a jab of violation by his casual entry into her places of privacy and the way he was doing it. With a scheduled inspection, you had time to make sure your spaces were in order. And, personal items like clothes weren't usually touched. He finally returned to where she was standing and took the coffee offered him. He took a seat in one of the chairs.

He took a sip and set the coffee on the desk. "I just wanted to come by to welcome you to the command."

"Thank you, sir," but neither his words nor his presence seemed terribly welcoming.

"You've had a lot of success so far, and I would like to see that continue."

Dee's mind was spinning, but she said nothing. *Where is this going?*

"This is your first, well, operational assignment, and although it is relatively small, each and every assignment is important for your career."

"Yes, sir, I understand."

"Good. From here, all promotions will be more and more selective, and I take pride that those who do well under my command have had good careers. Unfortunately, the services are traditionally a man's domain."

Her body tensed. Heat filled her face. Her heart was pounding. *Man's domain my ass!*

"But that is changing." He paused – for too long. "For the better. It's just important to remember that it may take more on the part of our female officers to be as competitive as some of the males – although it isn't right, of course. It is easy – in retrospect – at the end of our careers, to see those things we've done well and those things we either could have done better or, those things maybe we shouldn't have done at all."

Dee was silent. She didn't trust herself to speak. *What is he talking about?*

"Part of my job is to make sure you are counselled about what you should do, and maybe what you shouldn't as well. I take great pride in guiding junior officers to success. But, sacrifice, and doing things we may find difficult is part of the game. Of course, now a days, everyone is expected to give one hundred and ten percent."

"I'll do my best, captain."

"Yes, I know you will. I like your past record and I believe you will do well. I feel an obligation to mentor those who are success minded under my command – to give them a leg up, as it were, in their careers."

"Thank you, sir. I'm sure I will learn a great deal from your counsel."

"Yes, and I appreciate your willingness to take direction. I will, from time to time, provide guidance that will help your career, and your performance will be rewarded on my evaluations of you. I'm not a micromanager, but I hope you will take my direction to heart. I want to make sure I can count on you and in return, and I'll be happy to give you the evaluations you need."

"Yes, sir. Thank you, sir."

"I suppose I should be getting back to headquarters," he said standing, "but I'm glad I stopped by to say hello in person and I'm glad we had this little chat." He shook her hand, standing a bit closer than she thought he should. He held her hand as he looked around the room.

"It's a bit dated, but I have an idea that if you do well here and play your cards right, you may be moving up in the not-too-distant future."

Captain Trahir left, leaving the door open in doing so. Dee was left to parse the meaning of the visit. On the surface, it would seem he wanted to welcome her – although she didn't feel particularly welcomed. And, he'd offered to help her career along. But along with the offer came a few comments she found troubling. As a new lieutenant, she wasn't sure she should have questioned him, at least for now. Then, too, he'd had her make coffee and barely touched it. *Was he just trying to hammer home who is in charge?*

She dropped into her chair. Man's world? First operational tour? He thinks I'm going to need to suck up to him to have a successful career. And who knows what the chief has in store for me. Something about learning the ropes. I wonder what that means. Am I strong enough for all this? Can I do this? That's what this is about isn't it? Is daddy right? Am I going to give up when it gets tough? *No. Sink or swim. I'm in all the way.*

Five

They were about half-way through the plant property inventory. Dee was surprised that Chief Jackson hadn't said anything when she'd said she wanted to repeat the process that had been completed a month or so before. He carried the clipboard and presented it when she wanted to look at any of the items, pointing out the next item to be inventoried. She was becoming uncomfortable with the silence.

"Oh, by the way. Before I got transferred from Cape May, I worked on and off with a friend of yours. George Pierce."

"Oh?" He paused for almost half a minute. "How is George? We've been out of touch."

"He's doing okay. He said I should tell you that it's been too long since you two have gone fishing."

He didn't respond immediately. "Fishing? Yeah. We had some great times."

"He mentioned a trip where you went out to catch a marlin. Instead, you got a rock cod. And he laughed about it." She looked over at him. He was staring at her oddly. "What are you thinking about?"

"Just thinking about the trip."

"Yeah. He mentioned it more than once. Something wrong?"

"No. Just thinking back. We went out ocean fishing, more than once. I was usually looking to get something big. Really big. One time, I got a small rock cod – by far the smallest thing of the day. He referred to it as my marlin."

It was a funny story, and he should have been smiling, but he wasn't. In fact, there didn't seem to be any emotion in the telling. Instead, he looked lost in thought. *Why?*

"So," he said, "tell me about your last assignment."

"Admiral's aide." They stopped and turned toward each other. The sun was in his face. Dee's eyes moved constantly over their surroundings. *Why don't I want to look at him while I talk?* "When I got the job, I was really thrilled. After about a month, I found out I was basically his personal assistant. I made appointments, screened callers, made reservations, that sort of thing. I became disillusioned with what I was doing – my contribution to the security of the country. That's when I met your friend and he suggested I might find the operational side better than the administrative side. If I'd waited much longer, I would have been too senior to change."

They had just about finished with the list and started back to the offices. She spotted a jet ski inside the hangar. She ran her finger down the master list but didn't find it.

"Yeah, that's from up the coast. They actually have four – and only use two. So, the chief up there wanted to send this one down here. He said it has issues from time to time. I'm better with mechanical stuff than he is. He's using our expertise. We're doing maintenance on it and extended testing to make sure it's running right."

"Extended testing."

"Yup."

"Sounds more like you're borrowing it. It isn't ours. Is that going to be a problem?"

"No. I'll just keep doing the maintenance, checking it out, and logging it." They entered the hangar. "Coffee, ma'am?"

"Uh, yes, please."

"What do you take?"

"Two creams and half a Splenda."

He returned with two mugs and handed one to her.

"So, we're about finished. Anything else I need to see?" she asked.

"Two of the items," he twisted his head to see the clipboard which was now in her hands, "numbers 17 and 22, were surveyed. Copies of the paperwork are attached underneath. Then, you'll just have one piece of electrical gear which is out for testing and a vehicle that is currently in the shop in town having routine maintenance. I can have everything typed up for you."

"Thank you." *What was the deal was with the fishing trip? His friend made sure I knew it was important and that I mention it. It should have been funny, but he was just staring at me.*

Six

Dee walked down to Annie's office with the plant property inventory sheets in hand. Annie was doing something on her computer. Dee gave a courtesy knock on the door, then entered and settled into one of the chairs.

"How'd the inventory go?" It was professional Annie. Her hair was in a pony tail. Dee thought it made her look much younger.

"Okay. Everything seems to be here, including a couple of things that maybe shouldn't be. They aren't on the inventory."

"Did you ask him?"

"About a jet ski. He said he's helping out a friend by doing the maintenance. I don't know. I thought I'd check everything over twice and see what items turn up. If not, then I'll ask."

"Sounds good. I'm sure the chief has everything on the up and up, or at least covered by adequate paperwork." Annie took a sip of coffee from a mug and shuffled through some papers on her desk. "On a different note, the mandate for the annual physical fitness test came down from headquarters. I looked through your records and see you haven't done yours. They're doing it here in a couple of days. Shall I add one more to the list?"

"Sure. Why not?"

"Okay. Instead of the run, they usually do a swim – chief says we work on the water, everyone should be in pretty good swimming shape. That good for you?"

"Uh, sure. Why not? I can swim."

"I'll let him know. They do it off shore. A hundred yards out, then back." She said it as if a two-hundred-yard swim in the ocean was routine.

Two hundred yards? In the ocean? Doesn't sound like it will be easy, but I should be okay. *I feel tired just thinking about it.*

"As a matter of fact, they're doing the prelim today. Don't want to miss that." Annie smiled.

"Why? And, what prelim?"

"For the swim itself, there will be someone on the start/finish to make sure everyone who goes in comes out. And, there will be two people on a jet ski along the route, in case anybody gets into trouble. So, the prelim is basically a race between the two who will be on the jet ski. I'm the start/finish checker."

"A race?"

"Yeah. The chief and whoever else is going to be on the jet ski. For the race today, they start from where everyone else starts and swim out to the jet ski, which will be about a hundred yards off shore. For this particular swim, the jet ski will be slowly motoring toward Hawaii, so the person to reach it first won't have to swim as far as the one who reaches it second. Then, it's a race back to the starting point. If the chief wins, the enlisted have to pay for the party after the group PT. But if whoever else finishes first, the chief pays. Quite a party, too."

"So, how often does the chief win? And why don't we want to miss it?"

"To answer both of those, you're going to have to see the event. Come on!" Annie popped out of her chair and headed for the door.

Seven

They left Annie's office and headed outside. It was a sunny afternoon. The ocean was a beautiful blue. A light wind kicked up waves more than a foot high. *That's going to make the swim more difficult.*

The enlisted troops were relaxing, apparently waiting for the swim to start. The females seemed to be clustered in twos and threes close around the starting point. At least a hundred yards off shore, the jet ski moved back and forth. *That's a hundred yards? Now, I'm getting worried about this swim.*

The chief and another man left the building and headed for the starting point. They wore swimming trunks and t-shirts. They were laughing and joking. Dee noticed that the chief had a build somewhere between a swimmer and a gymnast. He was tan and – if she weren't an officer, she would say – gorgeous. *You know. For a guy. For an enlisted guy.* She shook her head to clear the thoughts. She noticed the female enlisted and Annie, as well, watching him like they were memorizing every muscle and curve.

One of the enlisted men yelled, "Hey, Ayala, do us proud."

The second competitor, no slouch in the body department himself, gave the man who yelled a thumb's up. He looked to be ten years the chief's junior.

They stepped on the pier and walked to the end. They removed their shirts and shoes. The "judge" for the race was talking, "No biting or scratching. No blows below the belt. In the case of knockout, the standing competitor will go to a neutral corner."

"They find a way to make a farce of it," said Annie.

The two lined up at the edge of the pier.

Why do I feel nervous? It doesn't really matter who wins – does it?

There was the sound of a whistle, and both men dove into the ocean. Dee started to edge toward the water. Ayala was swimming well. Strong. His hands made small splashes as they dug into the waves. The chief was parallel to him, maybe a bit behind. His stroke was also strong and, she thought, incredibly smooth. There was no wasted effort, and not even a small splash as his hands entered the water. *He isn't old by any means, but can he keep up with the young guy?*

I took a few minutes for the two to reach the receding jet ski. By the time they reached it the distance had grown to almost a hundred and fifty yards.

Come on chief. Come on. Why do I feel that way?

Ayala reached it first, touched the stern and turned for home. The chief was about five yards behind, but before he could reach the water craft, the driver goosed the throttle, pushing him ten yards farther out.

"That's not —" she said trying not to shout it out. *Damn thing is fifteen yards farther out now.*

The chief touched the jet ski and turned for home, now almost twenty-five yards behind the leader.

Ayala was swimming for all he was worth; his arms and feet churning the water. Dee was sickened. He'd been cheated. *Come on! Come on!* But she deflated because there was no hope.

Then, she was amazed to see that the distance between the two swimmers was closing. While his strokes were still picture perfect, they were coming faster, and faster. He was closing, but would there be enough time? *Come on! Please! Come on!*

They were fifty yards out. He might just make it. Might. "Come on!" she yelled. She would have been embarrassed, but everyone was yelling. Some for Ayala, some for the chief. She looked at Annie. Annie was clapping and laughing.

Twenty yards out, he caught Ayala. Ayala was tiring. *Yes!!!* At fifteen, he was a head in the lead. At ten, half a body length. "Yes!! Go!"

At five yards, he rolled over on his back and stopped swimming. Ayala passed him and touched the pier first. "No! No!" Ayala was panting, trying to catch his breath. The chief skulled in next to him, breathing hard, but not as hard as Ayala.

"Looks like you beat me fair and square. I guess I'm paying for the party. Good race. Congratulations."

They loaded the whole thing against him, which he probably knew from the start. Then, he still won, and he threw it so he'd pay for the party. I'm beginning to understand. Then, to Annie, "So how many races has the chief won?"

"Never." She was grinning and bouncing up and down slightly. "Somehow, no matter how far in the lead he is, he always falters in the last five yards."

The jet ski returned and the rider tied it up, then started to walk away.

"Pritchett!"

There was no response.

"Hey! Pritchett!"

The Coastguardsman turned. "Oh. What chief?"

"Problem with the throttle out there, or were you trying to hedge a bet?"

"What?! Me? No. Something just happened."

"We wouldn't want that to happen again, would we? I mean with the swim in the next couple of days. If somebody got into trouble, we wouldn't want the throttle to act up. Tell you what, why don't you stay this evening and we'll take the entire throttle assembly apart, you know, just to make sure it doesn't happen again."

The Coastguardsman named Pritchett turned and walked away with his head hung low.

"You know there isn't anything wrong with that throttle," said Ayala.

"Yup, but he'll be here until midnight making sure."

Both laughed.

Eight

Dee sat in her office with Annie and Chief Jackson. Each held the budget sheets for the previous and upcoming fiscal years.

"Okay. I don't understand this line item 95T. There's a lot of money in here, and I don't see where it went. The money just seemed to disappear."

"Yeah," he said. "That was a discretionary fund used by the OIC. It was created for various things that were of interest to him."

"Like?"

"I think he had some memberships."

"Memberships? What memberships? You're holding back."

"He used it for a country club membership, I think, and other things. Entertaining. Said it was to advance the reputation of the service."

"That's crap! It's basically a slush fund. And it's illegal. He could be prosecuted."

"Well, when he left here, he left the service. He'd have to be brought back on active duty to prosecute. That's very hard to do."

"I can't believe it!" said Dee.

"The fund, in part, was supposedly used to buy the new furniture for this office." It was Annie. "There were legitimate items proposed, it's just that the items proposed weren't the ones the money went to. There were apparently other priorities."

"This stuff is old and beat up. He stole money." Dee shook her head as she said it. "Said he used it for something legitimate and took it for personal use. I can't believe he did that." She looked at them.

"He was the boss," said Scott. "I've been in places where similar things were done. Usually, it's the whistle blower who ends up suffering."

"Okay. So, now I'm the boss. What needs to be done around here that we can use this money for? I assume that if we don't use it, they take it away - now and for the future."

Okay. She understands what went on and she's going to correct it. Got to give her props for being honest. "Yes. We could do the needed upgrades on our computers," he said.

"Or, get new furniture for this office," Annie said with a head tilt and a smile.

"Okay. Computer upgrades. Anything else? Training?"

"It would be nice to get some of the enlisted to additional first aid or medical treatment courses," said Scott.

"We've got three individuals who are going to school at night – to get their Bachelor's," he continued. "You might consider giving each some reimbursement."

"Okay. Good. How is the coffee mess funded?"

"Everybody kicks in," he said.

"So, let's make that a station function. The least we can do is help keep everybody awake. Might want to get something for those who don't drink coffee. Anything else?"

There was a pause.

"Good. I think that should take up most of it. We can decide what else we could do if we find we have money," said Dee.

"You might also consider buying additional ammunition and make sure everyone is up to speed for their firearm quals," he added.

"Good thought. Meanwhile, I guess, PT tomorrow."

"Yes, ma'am."

Nine

Dee was sitting on her office floor, in a matching blue sweat suit. She was weak and worn out – and sweating.

"Not bad," said Annie. "Forty-one push-ups and fifty-four sit-ups. Want me to pad that a bit? Right now, that's decent, but a few more in each column and you'll get into the 'excellent' categories."

"Pad them? No. I'll take my score honestly. Anybody else ever ask you to pad?"

"The last OIC. Supposed to be the honor system, but he said he didn't want the chief to look that much better than him. Actually, I'm glad you declined."

"He didn't want the chief to look better? How much better?"

"Well, the chief usually pops off a hundred or so push-ups and sit-ups."

"It's only two minutes for each!"

"Yeah." Annie said it quietly, turned her head and looked out toward the group assembled near the bay.

"Okay," said Dee, rolling onto her knees and struggling to her feet, "time for the next round."

They left her office and walked outside. Annie donned a beige straw sun hat. The chief was standing on the pier with a clipboard. Annie walked up to him and stood close to see what was on the clipboard. She wore pleated, white, wide-leg shorts that came to about mid-thigh and a white short-sleeved shirt. Annie's shoes were straw wedge sandals with a bow tie over each of the toes. Everything fit perfectly. *I wish I could wear something other than khaki every day.*

"We'll do relays of four," he started. "That way it will be easier to keep eyes on everybody. Then, we'll do the two at the end – like we usually do." He called out four names, Dee was among them. "Okay, you will be the first four. Out and back. I don't know everyone's skill level, and if you aren't used to ocean swimming, it isn't like you are in a pool. Take it easy and pace yourself. Everybody gets a good time. All you have to do is finish."

"Wouldn't it be warmer a little later?" one of the others asked.

"The ocean warms over a long period, not a couple of hours. A few minutes this morning won't matter. Besides, the ocean currents bring in cold water all the time."

Glad I didn't ask. Would have showed how much I don't know.

"Besides," he continued, "by the time the last group finishes, the waves will be up a bit, and that will make swimming tougher. Other questions?"

There were none.

Dee walked to the pier and removed her sweats and sneakers. She rubbed her arms and legs to get rid of the goose bumps. She looked at the water, her arms and legs sluggish and heavy. *I'm not sure I'm up to a two-hundred-yard swim in the ocean today.*

Ten

Scott walked to the end of the pier and untied the jet ski. Ayala was walking toward him. When Scott turned, he saw Dee doffing her sweats. She was five foot six. But the way her slim figure looked in her swim suit caught him off guard. He was staring. He was trying not to, but he was. Her dark blond hair cascaded to her shoulders. She twisted it and was stuffing it into a cap. He was mesmerized by the way her arms moved, the way she twisted and flipped her hair into the cap.

Then, she was rubbing her arms and legs. Her skin was pale. *Probably cold. Well, it's going to get a lot colder in a minute. July or not.* His eyes drifted lower, to her breasts, waist, then legs. Her figure was perfect in every way he could imagine. Sensuous. He knew he shouldn't be looking. He knew he shouldn't be thinking what he was thinking – or feeling what he was feeling. But he was beginning to feel pulled toward her. He shook his head. *No. Not her. And why her, anyway? I'm not going to get involved. She'll be like the others. Got to fight any feeling. It's been a long time – I guess too long. Still, she's who she is, and I'm not going to trust her. And, what did that song say, a pretty face don't mean no pretty heart?*

Ayala turned and glanced in the direction of Dee. "New L T is kind of a looker, isn't she, chief?"

"Yeah. She's okay, but even just looking the wrong way is bad for a career." He was conflicted and he knew as he was saying it that it probably sounded hollow. He certainly didn't feel it. Unprofessional personal interactions – fraternization – between officer and enlisted were prohibited – punishable – and career ending. Still, something within him stirred when he saw her.

"It doesn't pay to get mixed up with them." It was Ayala. Then, "You want to drive?"

"Uh, yeah. Might as well."

"You okay, chief? You seem distracted."

"I'm good." With that, he mounted the jet ski, looked to make sure Ayala was secure on the sled behind, and headed out into the bay.

Eleven

Dee stood on the pier after removing her sweats and shoes. She'd stuffed her hair into a swim cap to keep it out of her way. She wasn't looking forward to diving into the cold ocean, but at least the waves were small, and it would be over soon. Better than sitting here anticipating it for the next hour or so. She looked over at the chief. He seemed to be staring in her direction. She hoped everything was in place. *Okay. I've got my suit on.* She ran her hands over her swim cap. *No hair sticking out. What's he looking at?* She smiled. *Maybe it isn't me at all. Imagination.* But she had that feeling he was watching her. *Maybe it is me.* She double checked everything. *How much could be out of place if all you're wearing is a swimsuit? Nothing is hanging out.* She decided she wanted to look good if it was her he was watching. *Nice to be noticed, even if nothing is ever going to happen.*

"Okay, folks." It was Annie, bringing her back to reality. She checked the names of the first four. Like somebody was going to sneak in a substitute. "Out to the buoy and back. Take your time. Get back alive, you pass. Any questions?" She smiled.

"Everybody ready?"

Everyone nodded or mumbled they were.

"Don't expect a ready, set. Or a gunshot. GO!"

She dove into the water. The shock jolted her. *God it's cold!* She started to swim, fast at first, then remembering what the chief said, she backed off a little. *Don't want to tire and have to be rescued.* Wouldn't do for the OIC to set a bad example and get dragged out of the water like a spent tea bag. She noted with some satisfaction that their group was sticking together. But she was used to swimming in a pool, and this was tougher. She timed a breath wrong and caught a mouthful of water – salty water. She coughed and sputtered, stopping for a minute, treading water while she cleared her airway. She looked up and saw the chief standing on the jet ski, his eyes glued to her. When she stopped coughing, he held up a hand, pointed to her, then made an "O" with his thumb and index finger. She returned the "okay" sign and resumed her swim.

She was a bit behind now but fought the urge to speed up and catch the other swimmers. It seemed to take forever, but she finally was within ten yards of the buoy at the turn-around point when one of the group members came past her on the way back. She was swimming fast. *Trying to impress someone?* Dee was the last in her relay to touch the buoy and head for home, her arms and legs heavy as lead. She was breathing hard. The cold she'd felt earlier was dampened by a full body numbness.

The jet ski started to move – fast – heading for a spot not quite half-way back. She started treading water to see what was going on when Ayala dove into the sea. A few seconds later, he pulled the group speedster out of the water and put her on the sled. She was coughing up water but appeared to be okay otherwise. The watercraft continued to shadow the remaining members of the group.

Dee was second to last – or middle swimmer – in her group after one of the other two tired and slowed dramatically. The jet ski shadowed the slowest. She finished her swim and stayed in the water, not trusting her arms or legs yet for the short climb up the ladder. As she panted by the pier, trying to catch her breath, a shadow crossed over her.

"Give me your arms." It was the chief, bending down, reaching for her with his arms straight out but crossed at the elbows.

She reached up. He took her hands in his – strong hands – and lifted her. As she came up, his arms untwisted so she spun half-way around and came to a sitting position on the pier.

"Thank you."

"My pleasure." He helped her to her feet. "I thought you might have been in trouble for a minute, but you handled it well. And, didn't try to catch everyone. That was smart. Johnson wanted to show off, but she ran out of steam way too soon.

"Is she okay? You had to pull her out."

"She's okay. Swallowed some water and didn't do as well with it as you did. She's feeling a little sheepish. Coffee?"

"Don't you have to go back out – for the others?"

"It will take a minute to set the next group up. There's time."

41

"In that case, yes. Thank you." A current of delight – maybe something else she was trying to deny ran through her at the thought of him getting her coffee. *Nice to be noticed*, she repeated silently to herself. "Two cream and half a Splenda, please."

He returned a couple of minutes later and handed her the cup. He also had a large towel that he handed to her. "There you are, ma'am, two cream and half a Splenda. I'd better get back to it." But he lingered another thirty seconds before heading back to his duty. He looked like he wanted to say something that he couldn't quite get out. She held the towel in her hand instead of wrapping it around herself – until the chief had climbed onto the jet ski and rode out to guard the next batch of swimmers. Then, she set the coffee on a rock and slowly wrapped herself in the towel, thankful for the warmth.

Yup. A good-looking man. But the whole thing about comparing him to a piece of meat – well, that's just wrong. Thoroughbred, now that I can accept.

The rest of the swims went without incident. During the last couple of relays, trucks arrived. The food and drinks for the party were unloaded and set up by those who had completed the swim earlier. Dee, back in her sweats, started to help, but Annie cut her off. "The officer isn't supposed to do the manual labor in this event. You're like royalty." Coals were lighted.

The chief stood on a table. "Okay. Last event before the party. For those who are new, we've got a great party lined up. Westport will be taking any calls, so everyone can join in."

Everyone cheered.

"The only thing to decide is who will clean up afterwards. For that, we're going to have a race. One male. One female. The winner will sit back and watch as the other gender does the clean-up. Annie has randomly chosen –," he used his hand and arm to point to Annie.

"Petty Officer Pritchett for the boys, excuse me, males, and Petty Officer Swanson for the ladies."

The young man Dee knew as Pritchett and a young blond woman with an attractive figure went to the pier. Neither were smiling. This was going to be a race. *Randomly chosen my white patootie*, she thought.

"Okay. On my command, out and back. No interfering with the other or you will be disqualified."

Both stood with their toes curled over the edge. They were five feet apart.

"Ready."

They bent at the waist.

"Go!"

Both hit the water at the same time. Swanson stayed under longer. Pritchett was up and stroking. Swanson came up and started stroking, as well. Both the men and women left where they were and ran to the edge of the pier. Both swimmers were moving smoothly, it looked like Pritchett might be in the lead, if only by half a length. All the way to the buoy, he kept his lead. Everyone was yelling – mostly the men for Pritchett and the women for Swanson. The swimmers turned at the buoy, Pritchett two seconds before Swanson. They were both stroking hard. Swanson inched forward. Pritchett pushed harder and pulled slightly farther ahead. Swanson wasn't going to give up easily. Her strokes were coming faster. Half-way home, she pulled even. They were like two race horses heading for the finish line. Stroke for stroke. Neither giving up. Ten yards. Swanson was inches ahead. It would all depend on the touch. Then, it was over. A cheer went up. Swanson touched less than a second before Pritchett. The men would clean.

The jet ski was hauled out of the water and onto a trailer. Music started and everyone formed a line to get their food.

Twelve

Dee and Annie sat sipping tea just inside the hangar near their offices. The sun had almost completed its downward arc. The sunlight on pastel colored clouds was producing a dazzling sunset. The last of the cleanup was being completed. The chief was carrying trash bags to the dumpster. He was wearing a t-shirt, mid-thigh length, snug swim shorts, and sneakers.

Without taking her eyes off of him, Annie said, "You know, when I saw Ayala jumping into the water, I thought maybe you had a problem – or created one to get some, you know, attention."

"No way. First, it would have been the wrong kind of attention, thank you, and second, I didn't want to be the idiot OIC who couldn't finish the PT swim. Not good for the leadership image."

"Yeah. Now, Johnson will have to do the run. Those get timed pretty closely. And – *he*," she said with a nod to the chief, "won't be doing the timing. Nice try, though."

Dee looked around. "Seems like all the ladies, pretty much, stuck around. Just to see the guys clean up?"

"No. The party will likely go for a few hours after cleanup. The chief and a couple of others will stay sober and make sure those who aren't get a ride home."

They stayed quiet for a moment. Dee noticed some of the females engaging the chief in conversation. She turned to Annie and said, "Looks like you might have some competition. I mean you'd be pretty hard to beat today with the outfit you're wearing. Still."

Annie snorted. "They don't have a chance. He can see even subtle attempts from a mile off. It's kind of cute to see him deflect those. For the not-so-subtle ones he has a private talk with the young lady. He lets them down easily enough, but I've never seen a second not-so-subtle attempt from the same woman. And, what do you mean? This old thing? I just wore something suitable for an outing and picnic." She wiggled in her chair.

"Uh huh. I'm surprised some of the guys didn't walk off the pier while they were ogling you."

"I just like to look nice. And, if it gets a little attention, well, it's nice to dream. Don't think anyone is going to land that fish," Annie said with a nod toward Scott.

"You sound like an expert. Is this your hobby?"

"No. Just watching." Annie leaned in and lowered her voice. "But I know there was that woman in his past – you know, the wife. Something went bad, bad, bad." She sat for a minute. "Wouldn't mind knowing what the secret key is though. Be fun to throw that hunk of beef on the grill and –"

Dee flushed. "Would you stop referring to him as a hunk of meat. We don't like it when guys refer to us that way – and it just sounds – barbaric."

"Barbaric is what I had in mind," said Annie with a broad smile. "Really barbaric. Like where everything is sore for a week after. You know? And, I've found that when a woman objects to a particular guy being, what's the word?"

"Objectified?"

"No, but that will do. So, when a woman objects to a particular guy being," she turned and looked at Dee with a faux sweet smile plastered on her face, "objectified," she turned back, "it's usually just before said female starts stalking him herself. N'est pas?"

"Don't be ridiculous," Dee said as she straightened in her chair. "Even if – even if I were interested, as you say – and I'm not – you probably know that any nonprofessional activity between us if strictly forbidden. It wouldn't be smart, to say the least. Career ending not smart. And, I'm not about to ruin my career."

"Oooooo! 'Activity.' Is that what we're calling it?" Her eyes were wide. "How clinical. More like bungle in the jungle. And haven't you heard; love isn't just blind. It's stupid, too."

Just then, the chief bent over to pick something up. They had a view from directly behind. Then, he stretched up to put it on a shelf.

"I give that an eight," said Annie. "Ten if he'd been naked, but that's what dreams are for."

"Could we get on to another topic, please?" She knew she sounded desperate to change the subject, but she'd also watched every movement the chief made. And there was that heat again. She looked quickly at Annie. *I hope she hadn't seen me looking.*

"Fine," she said it like it wasn't. "I don't have anything else on Scott's – oh, pardon me – you know him more formally as the chief. I don't have anything else on him – yet. I guess it's time to pry into your background."

"Nothing to tell," she said too quickly.

"God! I'd LOVE to play cards with you someday. You're terrible at hiding things. It almost takes all the fun out. Almost. So. Give."

"There's nothing to tell. Really."

"I could play twenty questions," Annie said as she turned to look at Dee with a mischievous look. "As bad as you are at hiding things, I'll probably have sexual positions by question twelve."

"Fine." She'd said it with the same disagreeable tone as Annie had earlier. Both women laughed. "There was a guy. We dated for about two years."

"Then he cheated?"

"No."

"He died?"

"No. Do you mind if I tell this story?"

"Sorry."

"He actually was quite good looking. We're about the same age. He had a great job –VP for a large company in New York. Made great money, which his whole family had, as well."

"If he's still alive, can I have him?"

"Shush! He took me to Paris – over a weekend – and asked me to marry him."

"That Bastard!"

Dee looked at her like she was the child who had just said something incredibly stupid. "It would have been perfect, but – he started talking about how wonderful our lives would be. Big house in the Hamptons. On the water."

"Sounds terrible."

"Yeah, well, I was going to stay home. Have his two point five children. Stand behind the white picket fence – except it would have been so much more than a simple white picket fence in the Hamptons. Walk the dog. Be a part of the wives' club. Make sure dinner was ready every night. Cocktails on the lanai." She paused, closed one eye and cocked her head. "I wonder if it's still called a lanai in the Hamptons."

"Could be worse."

It took Dee, lost in the lanai question, a few seconds to respond, "Maybe, but it became clear as the 'discussion' went on that I was just another piece of what he wanted in his life. It didn't matter what I wanted. Money and house were supposed to be enough. So, I turned him down. He couldn't fathom the fact that I might want to do something with my life that was more than being his appurtenance."

"Appurtenance?"

"Yes. Look it up. Anyway, he wanted me to leave the service and do his bidding. I decided I'd rather be alone than live that kind of life. I'm not putting it down. If that is what a woman wants, more power to her. I want my footnote in history to reflect more than that. That's one of the reasons I really wanted this position. I'm doing something. And, it's pretty far from the Hamptons – and from a guy who showed up uninvited on occasion after we broke up. Couldn't seem to understand why I didn't want his perfect life. And, I may have been the first time he didn't get what he wanted. He was like the child with the one toy he couldn't have." She paused and sipped her tea. "I don't know if this will last forever. Maybe something more interesting will come along, but for now, it's what I want. And if I happen to find someone who will take me as I am – and maybe can on occasion be a bit barbaric –"

"Ooooo. There is still life in you," said Annie smiling broadly.

"Yeah, but at this point it's only theoretical. The parts, if you know what I mean, are a little rusty. Lack of use."

"Tell me about it. I heard someplace that if you don't – you know, work out the equipment," Annie's eyes went back and forth between Dee's lap and her face while she emphasized those words. "for seven years, you're officially a virgin again."

"You need therapy."

"Sex therapy." And they were laughed.

They sat quietly. The cleanup was finished. Some of the enlisted were sitting having a final drink – or two.

The chief walked over. "Mind if I join you for a cup before I call it a night?"

"Please," they said in unison.

"Either of you want anything?"

"Um, no," they replied in unison.

When he retrieved a cup of coffee, he sat with them and asked, "Any interesting topics of conversation?"

"No. No," said Dee. "Just girl talk. You know." And she smiled.

Thirteen

Scott Jackson checked and double checked the 28-foot small response boat. He wanted to be sure it was working perfectly. He had a job he needed to do, and the boat would have to perform. He planned to have the new lieutenant learn breaching the surf and it wouldn't be an easy day.

But he was anxious, as well.

After checking the hull, he double checked the seat attachments and yanked on the restraints to make sure they were strong, he started on the twin 225 HP outboard motors. If one of those quit or hesitated during their exercise, it would be a disaster.

He'd do a few runs with some of the other senior petty officers, smaller waves. Those would be what they would have to breach on a routine basis. After all, if it gets really bad, I'll be the one taking the boat out. I'm not going to let any of my people go out alone. But she needs to learn how to handle the bigger ones. And what it takes.

He checked and rechecked the engines, then tested them. There. Ready to be wrung out and tested thoroughly. He smiled. That thought could about either the boat or the trainees. But there was also anxiety within him. The day was going to be challenging, with real danger.

Ayala walked up behind him. "What's up?"

"Going to do some surf breaching tomorrow."

"Supposed to be some storm waves. Could be dangerous."

"I know what I'm doing."

"I know you know what you're doing. The question is, should you be doing it?"

"It's a good time for training. We can breach the smaller waves in the sets."

"So, you gonna have her do the smaller ones, too?"

"What makes you think it's all about her? I'm taking some of the others out, too."

"Same size waves?"

"What do you mean?"

"Oh, I don't know. Take the enlisted out on the smaller waves. Maybe take the L T through the big ones. Scare the crap out of her. That'd make you feel like a real man, wouldn't it?"

"That's not the way you talk to the senior NCO. Maybe you'd like to take on some of the really big ones."

"Don't give me that senior NCO crap. We've been together way too long for that. Besides, I've been out on bigger than the ones we're going to get. You and me. Rolled that boat twice in the thirty-footer before we got her back. What are you going to do if you roll her tomorrow?"

"That's not going to happen. She may have to be in charge on a boat going out. She's going to have to know what to do and how to do it."

"Tell yourself whatever you need to, but you and I both know what – or who this is about."

"That will be enough, Petty Officer Ayala."

"Fine. Anything happens, you're going to have to be the one to answer for it – and live with it. Unless it really goes bad. Then, I guess you won't have to live with it." He turned and walked away.

Scott Jackson stared at nothing for a long time. It's about the job. It doesn't have anything to do with – She needs to know what the crews can handle, and what they can't. And what she can't. She'll be the one deciding on their lives. That's what this is about. But it was a rationalization. He wanted to see if she could take it.

He stood and walked to his small office before leaving for the night. Ayala stood across the hangar bay, staring at him.

Fourteen

The silver hull of the small response motor boat slammed into the twelve-foot wave, pitching Dee and Scott forward in their seats, against their harnesses. Her hand was almost numb from gripping the joy stick, and her muscles screamed for release from the constant effort to fight the battering they were taking. The powerful little boat climbed the wave. White water slapped against the port window. She ducked her head to avoid the wave which had been stopped by the plexiglass. The boat rocked and she started to move the helm.

"Straight ahead! Straight ahead!" he yelled.

Her hand held the helm firm. The bow continued to rise more steeply as the boat struggled to climb the wave. Her heart hammered in her chest. *Come on. Come on. Are we going to flip over?* She looked at him quickly. His face was impassive. *What's he thinking?*

Then, they were at the top, and over into the relative calm of the ocean beyond. The boat started to pick up speed. She let out a breath, surprised to find that she hadn't been breathing. She throttled back. The twin motors quieted and the boat slowed. She released the helm and opened and closed her hand in an attempt to make it relax.

"You did pretty well with that one. Let's do it again. After that you can play instructor and spot what I'm doing wrong and correct me."

"Really. I think I've got it. We can go back in." *Please.* The response sounded weak, even to her. There was a sudden sinking feeling within her.

"We're almost done."

She turned the boat around and headed back in, her arms shaky and weak. *I don't know if I've got the strength. He'll keep me out here until I fail. That's the point, isn't it? Well, I'm not going to let him win.* She took deep breaths, unable to rid herself of the feeling she couldn't go on. But she wasn't going to let him prove she couldn't do this. Once again, she pointed the boat to plow through the giant wave, fearing every second that she would do it wrong and they would drown. He gave no instruction or correction. *If I don't do it right, he won't help. Oh, god!* The final charge up the waves finished without incident.

Then, Scott took the helm, he playing the student and she the teacher. "You tell me what I need to do to correct my attack on the wave."

They started out. She saw the first waves he was breaching were not at their crest. He started toward the first.

"Straight into the wave," she yelled as he approached at an angle. He overcorrected and she corrected him again. They crested the wave without problem. The second time, she had to tell him to use more power. The third time, Scott seemed distracted and let the boat drift sideways toward the cresting wave. "Into the wave! Into the wave!" But he didn't respond to what she was saying. She grabbed the helm, spun the boat away from the wave, then completed the three-quarter turn heading straight for it. It was the biggest wave yet. Her muscles tightened and her eyes were glued to the wave. Up and up they went, the motors churning at full power. The boat was pitching up at a dangerous angle. Dee's eyes were wide, the feeling of trouble building inside her. Then, they were over the top and out onto the calm of the ocean. Relief washed over her as she pulled back on the throttle.

"Not bad," he said, and after a two second pause, "for a girl."

Anger pulsed. She flipped the joystick hard left and hit full power. The boat's stern flashed around. She heard a 'thunk' as Scott's helmeted head crashed into the side of the boat.

She turned to look at him and with a wan smile said, "Oops. Did I do that?"

He was laughing. "Touché, and well played, by the way." He laughed again. "You did very well. No disclaimers. I wondered how you'd do on the last one, but you handled it perfectly. You didn't have time to turn into the wave, and you might have outrun it, but you gave yourself enough room by making the 270. Nice job."

"Do you mind if I ask why you put me through this? The others you brought out this morning only did a couple of approaches. And none of the other stuff."

He paused. "You're the OIC. You'll be the one who decides to risk the lives of your men and women. The lives lost could be either the ones in trouble at sea, or your charges. Tough call to make, who lives and who dies. You've got a better idea now what a crew might have to go through. You'll give the order for them to stay or go. Then, too, you're probably going to be going out on some of these calls. If something goes wrong with the approach to a wave, they're going to look to you to make it right. There's only one way to really know how to make it right. But you've got to keep in practice."

"But you'll be the one going out."

"Maybe not all the time, and I won't be here forever. And, well, suppose, just suppose, somebody moves the helm and power the wrong way, and I get knocked out when my head hits the side of the boat. You never know."

Heat filled her face. She was blushing.

"By the way, how did that last one feel?"

"Now that you ask, I guess I didn't have time to be scared. I just did it. I kind of wondered whether we'd make it, though."

Scott just smiled. He opened his mouth as if to say something when the radio crackled. "Chief. Got a couple of MMTBs about five miles out – mayday with their boat sinking. Well, slowly filling with water anyway. Since you're already out, do you want to take a look?"

Scott looked at her, and she nodded 'Yes.'

"We'll head out. Where are they?"

The dispatcher gave the location.

"You want to drive, Lieutenant?"

"Sure. Why not. Just as long as we don't have any 12-foot breakers to go through." She smiled.

They headed in the direction given to them by the dispatcher and rode in silence for a few minutes. Then, she said, "By the way, what did the dispatcher mean by MMTBs?"

"Uh, just, it means more money than brains."

"Wha –?"

"Usually doctors, but a lot of others, too. Rich people. They buy big, complicated boats – or airplanes, and don't have any idea how their toys work. When something goes wrong and they get into trouble, they don't know what to do and usually end up in real danger. Or dead." Then, "There, I think we've got our sinking boat."

She slowed and pulled the response boat close to a thirty-foot Viking cabin cruiser that appeared to be sitting low in the water. Three middle-aged or older men were standing on the open deck.

"Howdy, folks. What seems to be the problem?" asked Scott.

"Thank god you're here. The boat is sinking. I noticed some water in the bottom, so I opened that valve that lets the water out. That seemed to make it worse, so I closed that, but the motor is flooded and we can't get back. You need to pull us home." He was the oldest of the three and it was clear he had been drinking.

Scott looked at Dee and said, "Put me aboard and let me take a look."

She pulled alongside the pleasure boat, and Scott jumped aboard. He disappeared below, then returned a few minutes later.

"Well, sir, it seems whoever used the marine toilet didn't close the inflow valve completely. Then, that valve you opened to empty the water, only empties the water when the boat is completely out of the water. On dry land. When the boat is in the water, that valve lets water flow into the boat."

"Nobody told me that when I bought the boat. I should sue them. But that can wait. Right now, I need to have you get rid of some of that water and tow us back to shore."

Scott hopped back into the response boat. "I'm sorry, sir, but we aren't authorized to do either of those things."

"No. You've GOT to help us. That's why I pay taxes."

"Sir, we'll call a marine services business and have them come out. They will have dewatering equipment and a boat large enough to tow you back to shore."

"What! How much is this going to cost me? I pay taxes so you will take care of me when I need help."

"Sir." It was Dee. "We will stay on station until the other boat arrives, but we do not have the dewatering equipment they have and I am not going to hazard this boat by towing yours. Neither is an authorized part of our mission."

"What!" It was the man on the cabin cruiser. He looked at Scott and said, "Are you going to let that – that *girl* tell you what to do?!"

"What I'm going to do, sir, is what the lieutenant directs."

"A girl officer? What is the world coming to?"

"A lieutenant, sir. And, she is in charge. If you like, you can wait over here until the marine services arrives."

The men on the yacht talked among themselves, then, "Okay. We'll come over." The oldest-looking picked up two six packs of beer and headed for the response boat.

"I'm sorry, Sir," said Scott, "but the alcohol will have to stay on your boat."

He looked shocked. "I suppose that's her order," pointing toward Dee.

"If it were, I would obey it, but the truth is, it would be against regulations. I would suggest that you might want to abstain until you are back in port."

"Never mind. We'll stay here." Seemingly in defiance, he passed a beer to each of his friends and made a show out of opening his.

Scott turned to Dee and quietly said, "When I retire, I'm going to write a book based on my experiences. I'm going to title it, Morons with Boats."

Dee turned away to cover her laugh in response.

They waited until the boat from the marine salvage business arrived and had the situation in hand. Then, they departed.

When they were clear, she said, "Thank you for your support back there."

"My pleasure, but it wasn't anything special. You *are* the officer in charge."

"Well, I appreciate it, anyway." She was silent for a minute, then, "And, while you scared the hell out of me this morning, I guess I should thank you for that, too."

"Everything is hard until it is easy. You did well, and it is something you need to be able to do."

She looked at him. She was seeing him differently. He was the guy who knew how to do everything operational, but there was more to him than that. He'd challenged her today, but he'd also taken care of her. She could see why his people – well, they were her people too – were so loyal.

Fifteen

"So," she started, "do you get many of those calls, you know, people who do stupid things and get themselves into trouble?"

"I'd say you'd be amazed, but you'll be reviewing all the calls, so it won't take you long to find out that a lot of people who buy or rent a boat and go on the ocean out don't have a clue. I'm surprised we don't have more serious incidents than we do."

They approached the pier. She turned the helm and allowed the boat to bump the structure lightly.

"Good. Nice job."

"Thank you. As long as you don't have any qualifiers to add."

"I learned my lesson, thank you. Besides, I'd never say anything where someone might hear and think I meant it." He jumped from the boat to the pier and tied the boat's bow. Then, he tied the stern. He offered his hand to her and helped her out of the watercraft.

"I think I'm going to shower before doing anything else," she said and turned to walk to the hangar. As she opened the door to her office, she noticed him in the reflection of the glass – watching her. She smiled. *Not a bad day. That exercise in the surf wore me out. I didn't want to admit that it really scared me. I wonder if that was the point. At least I didn't let him know I didn't think I could do it.*

Fifteen minutes later, she emerged from her private room, freshly washed and in a clean uniform. Yes, she was supposed to be a rough and tumble Coast Guard officer, but it still felt nice to be clean.

She sat at her desk, looking over messages until 4 o'clock. Then, she walked down to Annie's office, only to find it empty. She called to one of the petty officers working on a boat, "Have you seen Annie?"

"Uh, no. Not for a while."

She walked out of the hangar and around the side to where the reserved parking was located. Annie's spot was empty.

"Darn it!"

"What's up?" It was the chief.

"Oh, nothing. It's just – well, I was going to drop my SUV at the shop tonight. It needs routine servicing and I want them to look at a couple of other things. She was going to give me a ride home after I dropped my vehicle."

"No problem. I can take you. Give her a call when you get home and see if she can pick you up in the morning. If not, call me and I'll give you a lift in, as well."

"Uh – okay. I just need to get my things."

"It will take me a couple of minutes to change. Why don't you give me the name of the place, and I'll pick you up there then run you home? It'll take you a few minutes to do the paperwork."

"Okay." She dug in her pocket and pulled out a business card with the name of the shop. He photographed it with his mobile phone. Dee went to her office and packed up her things. She walked out, climbed into her SUV, and headed for the dealership. She rolled down her window and let the ocean breeze blow through the car.

I wonder what happened to Annie. She knew I needed a ride. Hope it isn't serious. But if it's not, why leave?

The ride went quickly and before she knew it, she'd arrived. She checked in with the manager, filled out the form, and was turning to walk out, when a red pickup arrived. *1940s?* The same one that had stopped on the coast highway that first day – a month and a half ago. Every head in the place turned to look. The truck was old but pristine. From the throaty sound of the engine, it was not original. The truck stopped. Scott Jackson got out. Stone-washed jeans, a University of Wyoming sweatshirt, and cowboy boots were his attire. It didn't take long before a group of onlookers circled the truck.

"Well, you certainly know how to make an entrance," she said smiling as she walked up to him.

"Yeah. You'd think nobody has ever seen an old truck." He walked to the passenger side and opened the door for her.

Individual seats were done in leather, light beige. The headliner and carpet were the color of coffee. The dash insets were wood, birds-eye maple, polished to a high shine. It was immaculate.

"I'm afraid I'll get it dirty. Would you prefer I ride in back?" she asked with a smile.

He gave her a disapproving look. "It's a vehicle. I redid it. I keep it clean. But it is meant to ride in."

She put her case behind the passenger seat and slid in. The seat was one of the most comfortable she ever experienced. "Where did you get these? They're incredible."

"A guy I know makes chairs for private luxury jets. I did him some favors. He made me the chairs. Yes, they are nice." He closed her door, walked to the driver's side and slid in. The engine came to life, a soft purr. "Now, how do we get to your place?"

She gave him the address. "I hate to have you go out of your way. I could –"

"Hitch hike?" he laughed. "Please. It isn't any problem. Don't forget your seat belt." Then, he backed out of the lot and turned onto the road. The soft purr became subdued throaty roar as the truck accelerated and she was pushed deep into the soft, engulfing seat.

They rode in silence for a few minutes, then she asked, "So, what are your plans after this – this assignment?" *I hope he'll say he's going to stick around awhile. Could make my life easier. Seems like a good guy, and you never know who will replace him. Maybe somebody who will make my life worse.*

"I'm not sure. I like it where I am for now. I don't know what I might want to do. Well, actually, there is a small family business."

"So, and don't get me wrong, I looked at your file – like I did with everyone – and with your record, you could have been a senior or master chief by now. But you never tried."

"And you want to know why." He stopped his scan of the road for a second, turned and smiled quickly at her.

She just sat, wondering what to say, hoping she hadn't touched a nerve.

"The truth? Making senior or master would have required me to do things I didn't want to do. I wouldn't be the senior NCO at this small station. I'd be at a large facility, shuffling papers, sitting in meetings, talking to people I don't particularly like about things I don't care about. They're all trying to get ahead of the next person. I don't need it. I'm out here having fun, running through breakers with the new OIC." He looked at her again and smiled. She liked his smile.

She wasn't sure how to respond. Most people she knew wanted more and did things they didn't particularly like to get where they thought they should be. Here was a man who knew what he wanted and was happy with less – whatever that meant – to have the life he preferred.

"How about you?" he asked. "You came from the big house to a small station. Mind if I ask why?"

"I decided to change my career path. After I graduated from college, I was assigned as an assistant logistics officer."

"Box kicker," he said with a smile.

She smiled in return. "Not even head box kicker. I was a junior box kicker. I had a lot to learn." She looked at him. "A LOT to learn. The man in charge had a plan for the annual inspection."

"It's a big deal," he said.

"You don't have to tell me. Anyway, he kept me well informed about what had to be done. He not only wanted my help, but he wanted to give me information to help my career. Then, a month before the inspection, his gall bladder blew up on him. I was left to complete the preparations for the inspection."

"That must have been tough."

"Not so bad. I had a great plan – his plan, and good people, as well. We did great. The admiral was impressed. When I told him it was all the result of someone else's plan and the execution by a great staff, he said, "Just what all good officers do – give credit to everyone else." In this case, it was someone else's plan. And I had a lot of help. Anyway, I went from being an apprentice box kicker, as you say, to admiral's aide."

They arrived at her complex. "Oh, right over there. My unit is that one," she said pointing. There was a party in one of the units, and people, mostly male and mostly drunk, were wondering the grounds. Scott parked the truck and got out. He walked to her side and opened the door.

"No need. I'll be fine," she said.

"I'd just rather see you get inside okay. I've got memories of parties like this and how fast things can get out of control when a beautiful young woman appears." He offered his hand to help her from the truck.

"Well, thank you for the compliment, but I should be okay." She felt a warmth within her when he said she was a beautiful woman. She might not have believed it coming from someone else, but the way he said it was different. It was an observation, it seemed it was without thought of a response or gain on his part.

"I know. Please. Just humor me." He put his arm on her shoulder as he moved them through a group of drunks. Some turned and watched her closely, then turned away when Scott gave them a warning look.

She knew the rules regarding fraternization, but decided she liked the feel of his arm on her. Besides, it was for safety. She told herself.

They walked around the building and to the staircase. She led the way up.

"I'll be fine now."

"Please. I'd like to make sure you're inside okay."

A drunk bumped into them when they reached the top of the stairs. She was pushed backwards, and he caught her in his arms. The shock of falling and the short-lived fear of the drop was replaced by something she hadn't felt in a long time that swirled within her. Scott pushed the drunk backwards against the wall with his left arm and held him there.

"Hey! Whata ya tink yur — " he slurred.

"You're drunk. Go home."

"You cana tell me what a do."

"Then stay out of our way."

She was still pressed against him. She knew she should be frightened by the obnoxious drunk, but she felt safe. And warm. And something else.

He walked her to her door. Slightly flustered, she looked through her purse for her keys. He was standing close. Very close. She realized she liked him close. *What am I thinking?* She looked up. He was scanning for threats, then looking at her – into her. She was flustered. That something else feeling was growing. She recognized it as desire. She looked into his eyes. *I wonder if I tilt my head back just a bit – would he kiss me?* It was silly and reckless. Annie's words ran through her head, *Love isn't just blind. It's stupid, too.* She was being stupid. She had a career to protect.

"Uh, I'm having trouble finding my keys. They're usually –"

"Take your time. I'm in no hurry."

But she was having trouble relaxing, caught between feelings of what she should do and what she hoped might happen. But, then, as she tried to work all that out, she found her keys. She turned and opened the door. "Uh, thank you. I, uh, appreciate the ride, and the, uh, protection." *Why am I having trouble finding words?*

"My pleasure. I want you to be safe. Why don't I swing by and pick you up in the morning? Seven? That way you won't have to worry about calling Annie and you'll be sure you have a ride."

"Uh, thank you. That would be nice. And, seven would be perfect. Good night."

"Good night. I'll wait to hear the door lock click before I go."

She closed the door and locked it, then threw the deadbolt. She collapsed with her back against the door. *What an idiot! I should call him and say I'll check with Annie. I'm glad I didn't invite him in. I can't imagine. He probably would have refused. But what if he didn't? 'Hi. Just come in for a minute.*

It's not a romantic thing.' It even *sounds stupid to me. Jesus, who knows?* She went to the refrigerator and poured a glass of wine. *I can't believe I came that close to messing up.* But as she sipped her wine, thoughts of what might have happened wouldn't leave her alone.

Sixteen

Scott heard the lock and the deadbolt engage. He stared at the door for half a minute before turning and walking away. He retrieved his mobile phone and dialed a number as he descended the stairs. After a brief conversation with the police, he punched the off button and returned to his truck. As he left the parking lot, police cars started to arrive.

It took about twenty-five minutes for him to reach his apartment. He pulled into the double garage, turned off the engine, closed the garage door with the remote, and sat staring. Okay. You have to give her what she's due. You pushed her farther than you'd planned. Those were some damn big waves. He smiled. Even scared you. I thought we were going to flip on that last one. Then, she did okay heading out to the call and didn't lose her professional demeanor when she was out there. She's got promise.

He went to his apartment, poured himself three fingers of scotch, and sat looking out his picture window at the ocean. She'd asked why you'd pushed her. Everything you said was true. He took a sip of the scotch, holding it in his mouth for a few seconds before swallowing. He'd expected her to do poorly. She'd held fast and not given up. He'd been surprised you how tough she turned out to be. Did I really hope she'd fail? Her? Or was Ayala right? Somebody else.

He sipped the scotch. *She makes you feel like you haven't felt in a long time? Is that it?* What bothered him more than what he wanted to do was what he might have done. She didn't invite you in. She wouldn't have done that anyway – she's an officer. Committed to her career. She wouldn't. But what if she did? I mean it would just be stepping in for a minute, nothing else. No, it would have been more. It would have been much more. For me anyway.

He downed the scotch and tried to go through a list of things that he wanted to get done the next day. He was distracted and upset with himself for being distracted.

Seventeen

Dee woke quickly, covered in sweat. She'd been dreaming. She was in a large ship that was being capsized by a huge wave. The wave was so big, she couldn't see the top. Fear gripped her. As the ship rolled over, she was thrown out and was falling through the air. She was flailing when arms caught her and a parachute opened. She drifted to the ground and into a field of wildflowers. She landed softly, and turned to see Scott next to her. He moved to kiss her and she responded, then fought saying, "We can't. It's against regulations." But she didn't mean it. That's when she'd awakened. *Love IS stupid. Well, it would be if this were love, but this isn't love.* It might not be love, but she was hot and sweaty from dreaming about him all the same.

She lay on her back, panting. When she looked at the digital clock, she saw it was 5:02. I've got an hour. I'm not sure I want to go back to sleep if another dream is waiting for me. But she drifted off, to be wakened at 6 AM by her alarm.

She showered and dressed, and had a bite to eat. At exactly 7, there was a knock on the door. She checked the peephole, saw Scott, and opened the door. She was having trouble looking at him, the dream still on her mind.

"Good morning. Right on time. Please come in while I gather my things? Would you like a cup of coffee?"

"Thank you, ma'am." He entered and stood just inside the door. He looked a little stiff. "And thank you for the offer, but we can get coffee at work. Save you from having to clean anything up here."

Is he acting more reserved than usual? Because he's in my apartment? I wonder if he had a dream last night. He looks pretty normal. Maybe it's just being in my apartment. Maybe I'm just seeing what isn't there.

"I just need to run something down the disposal." She ran the water and turned on the unit. "Dammit! Sorry. This thing isn't running right. Hasn't since I got here. I keep asking the manager to get it fixed, but he just doesn't do anything about it."

"Let me take a look," he said, stepping in.

"There's no need for you to. I mean they should fix what doesn't work."

"And, how's that working out for you?"

"Not very well, so far."

He pulled off his sweatshirt. "This shouldn't take too long – at least to see what's going on."

He was looking at the sink, in his t-shirt, and she was looking at his torso. She could only see his back, good thing, *if he knew I was ogling him – what am I doing? I should tell him I need to get to work*. She continued to stare, looking away quickly when he turned.

"Do you have a bucket I could use?"

"Uh, sure. I've got – there's one – I think I put it in the, uh, closet." *I sound like an idiot.* She went to the utility closet and pulled out a plastic bucket. "Uh, here."

"I'm just going to take a look under here." He opened the cabinet.

Thank god I straightened that two weeks ago. I would have been mortified. "Shouldn't we be getting to the station?" she asked weakly.

He pulled the items out of the cabinet and set them on the kitchen floor. "This shouldn't take too long," he said, as he crawled into the cabinet.

She was staring at his legs sticking out from her cabinetry. Images of her crawling on them began to form in her mind. *You're being an idiot! Stop!*

"If we can fix this in a short time, we won't be that late, and you won't have to swear at the manager every time you want to run something down the drain."

"I'll probably still swear at the manager." She said smiling and felt the tension drop, if only a bit.

After a couple of minutes he slid out from under the sink. "Why don't you call Annie. Tell her you will be a little late. I can have this fixed in an hour. I just need to run and get a couple of things. Won't take long, and the problem will be gone."

"I, uh, I'm not sure I should miss work, I mean, I'm supposed to be there."

"Tell her to say you're doing some off-site inspection if anybody asks. There won't be a problem. Even if somebody shows up, she'll cover."

"Sounds like you've done this before."

"Just one of the advantages of working at a small operational station." He smiled, grabbed his sweatshirt and headed for the door. "I'll be back in fifteen minutes."

Fifteen minutes later, he was back. And, in short order he removed the old disposal, snaked the drain, and put in a new disposal. She watched the entire time, her mind forming juvenile images of the two of them.

"Okay," her reverie was broken by his voice. "I want to show you something. I think you can get down here without getting dirty."

"Down there?"

"Yes, ma'am. Just slide in here on the other side."

She rose on shaky legs and went to the underside of the sink. "Can I see from here?"

"Uh, no. Here, just slide in," he gestured to the opposite side of the under-sink cabinet, "here."

Carefully, she maneuvered herself into the cramped space. She was less than six inches from him. He was clean shaven. She was staring at his skin. She smelled the faint fragrance of the soap he must have used. He spoke, and she looked into his eyes. *What if I kissed him? What if he kissed me? This is stupid. How did you two first kiss? Well, we were under the sink in my apartment. He was showing me the garbage disposal, and I couldn't resist. No. Stop. Stupid. Annie's right love is stupid. Even if this is only fantasy. It's stupid. Still . . .*

He finished explaining whatever he'd had her there to look at, not that she'd heard a word. She slid out of the cabinet as gracefully as she could. He slid out and put on his sweatshirt. She sighed, both in relief and for the loss of the view.

He checked that the unit functioned and didn't leak. Then he replaced the contents and closed the cabinet,

"Thank you. What do I owe you for all of this?"

"Not a thing ma'am."

"But you must have spent money on the disposal and other things."

"Please, don't worry about it. My pleasure."

She gathered her things. He stepped out onto the landing first. She followed and closed and locked the door. He preceded her down the stairs, then walked alongside her to his truck. He opened her door first, then when she was inside closed it and walked to his side and climbed in.

"Sleep okay?" he asked.

"Uh, yes, thank you." She remembered her dream and hoped he didn't see her start to blush as the heat returned to her face. "It quieted down not long after you left. I guess the party ran out of steam – or booze."

"Good. Sometimes those will get out of hand. Glad it didn't."

The old truck took bumps and turns like a luxury car. Again, the summer breeze tousled her hair. *I wonder if this is what it's like the entire year.*

"So, last night, you left off your story where you'd become the admiral's aide."

"Huh? Right. Well, that lasted about three years. At first, I was thrilled, you know, admiral's aide and all. It didn't take long to figure out I was a glorified executive go-for."

"Not your cup of tea?"

"I didn't consider it important work. I started wondering if he was going to have to hire someone when he retired. I wasn't sure he knew how to drive, get his dry cleaning, make reservations. Everything."

Scott was laughing.

"That's where I met your friend George Pearce. I got to know him and he listened when I said I wasn't doing anything important. He suggested I switch from an administrative track to an operational track. When my tour was up, the admiral said I could go anywhere I wanted – within reason. And, voila! Here I am."

She was enjoying the conversation while looking at the scenery and stealing glances at Scott when she could. She wondered about her dream and all those thoughts about 'what if' she'd invited him in. They arrived before she wanted the trip to end.

"Thank you for the ride – and the ride last night. I'll have to check with Annie and see what happened to her yesterday."

"Well, if she can't take you to the dealership tonight, let me know. I'll be happy to get you there."

She opened her door and left the vehicle before he could get out and around to her side. He accompanied her into the hangar.

"Coffee?" he asked.

"Yes, please," she answered ignoring the fact that she had a cup-maker in her office.

"Two creams and half a Splenda, as I recall. We've also got French Vanilla and Hazelnut, if you prefer."

"Yes. Thank you. You choose."

He returned a few minutes later with a stoneware mug. "There you are ma'am. I'd better get to my tasks for the day." He turned and left the office. She watched him walk away, still slightly embarrassed by her dream.

Eighteen

Annie entered and sat in one of the chairs facing the desk. Her legs were crossed and the shoe on her top leg was dangling from the toe, swinging as she rocked her foot.

"So, what happened to you last night? I thought you were going to run me to the shop, then home."

"Oh! I'm sorry. Was that last night?" The shoe stopped moving.

"Well, since I asked you yesterday morning, um, yes."

"I'm sorry if I left you in the lurch. Were you able to get a ride from someone else?" Annie was staring a hole in the carpet next to the chair, scratching the right side of her neck with her left hand.

"Why you – You did that on purpose! What did you think – why did you –?"

"So, no sparks? No fun?"

"Do you know how much trouble I could – he *and* I could be in if anything ever happened?"

"I don't know, I asked if you got a ride. I was wondering if it was a ride, or you know, a ride." Annie tilted her head forward and opened her eyes wide.

"Good lord, you must think we're like rabbits or something. Nothing happened. We exercised restraint."

Exercised restraint? That sounds terrible. Why am I having trouble talking?

"Restraint? Then there was something."

"That's not what I meant. Nothing happened. Nothing even approached happening. He walked me to my apartment and stayed outside my door."

"And, how did you feel about that?"

Heat pulsed in her face. "It was a ride home. There was nothing else."

Annie leaned forward, "Then how come you turned bright red when I asked how you felt?"

"I don't know what you're talking about."

"No thoughts? No regrets? Like, should I have asked him in for coffee – maybe a glass of wine? Did you ask him in?"

"No." She was glowing red now. It was as if Annie was reading her mind.

"Getting closer. Do you regret not asking him in? Think about what might have happened if you had? It's only fantasy. Even the Coast Guard can't prosecute you for fantasy." She sat for a moment, seemingly lost in thought. Then, "A dream? Yes, maybe a dream. Did you wake up sweaty?"

Dee dropped her eyes to the desk. She was starting to sweat. *How is she doing this?*

"Bingo! I told you – you are terrible at hiding things. I know it wasn't bad sweaty. It must have been good sweaty."

"Please! Stop!"

"Don't worry. Your secret is safe with me. I don't figure I've got a shot with him – which, by the way is a real tragedy, more so than something like the Chicago fire. I didn't think anybody had a shot – now *that* would be a tragedy."

Dee thought Annie must be lost on one of her tears. It didn't seem to matter if there was no one else in the room. The illogic train would roll on.

"And, I'm sharper than you might think," Annie continued. I've seen the way you steal glances. I also saw the way he was studying you before the swim."

"He was what?"

"He was memorizing you – from head to toe." She looked serious for a moment, as if trying to work something out. "It isn't lust – exactly. Something stickier. Something that gets into you and won't let go. Just like I've seen you do with him." She sat back and the seriousness was gone, "I thought I'd stir the pot a little. You know, I could almost hate you if you weren't so sweet."

"What?"

"Face it. Scott Jackson hasn't looked at a woman – I haven't seen it, anyway – since whatever happened with his ex. Then, you come along and Bam!"

"You're exaggerating.

"Am not. You're smart, strong, and gorgeous. He's smitten. Nobody else has come close. You're a goddess."

Dee stared for a minute, not believing what she heard. "I'm a *what*?! I hope nobody else heard that. They'll be laughing themselves silly."

"Wherever you go, I'll bet men are so distracted that they walk into things."

"Wherever I go, I see men yawning. I'm nothing special."

"I may have to take back the smart. You're probably so used to it you don't even see it anymore. Anyway, more to the point, I wanted to have him give you the ride."

"So, you left early. What if he hadn't been here?"

"I'd have given you a ride."

"How?"

Annie sat back. "I was parked on the other side of the building – and watching. I wanted to see what would happen. Anything intimate was too much to hope for, but my guess is his night was as disturbed as yours. You two are like teenagers, trying not to show you want something to happen but wanting it to all the same. Fun to watch. By the way, I noticed that you two – not just you – were about an hour late today. What gives?"

"Well, because *someone* didn't pick me up this morning,"

"Not that you actually wanted that particular someone to pick you up."

"When he got there, I was having trouble with that stupid garbage disposal that I've been trying to get the manager to fix. So, he said he'd take a look. That's all. He ended up fixing it for me. It took a little time."

"Wait. Oh, my, god. He checked out your plumbing?!" Her eyes open wide, she clapped her hands rapidly in front of her face like a child at a birthday party.

"Can you turn anything and everything into something sexual?"

"It's a gift. Besides, this one isn't even a stretch. So, he stuck his nose into your plumbing? Then, he poked around in it for over an hour and fixed the problem you've had for so long? You have no idea, this is priceless. I should write a book. I suppose he had to partially undress. Was that part nice? Did you stare? Of course, you did, especially if he was working and he couldn't see you staring. Were you like a teenaged girl and picture what it might be like? Did you help? I mean it *is* your plumbing. Maybe you held his tool while your plumbing got poked into." Annie giggled, obviously pleased with herself.

"Will you stop?!" But she was turning bright red.

"I'm sorry. I just wanted to have a little fun. I get so few chances. Did anything happen? I don't mean actual physical – um – you know, but you're upset. Was it too close? Too dreamy?"

"I'm glad you're having fun. Maybe it's been so long, I'm thinking about the first guy I've worked closely with. You can testify at the trial when they throw both of us out of the service and maybe into the brig."

"The danger is what makes it all the more exciting – not that I want to see either of you caught or thrown out. If anything happens, I'd like to see it last. But you might as well face it. You're both caught in the whirlpool. It's only a matter of time. As the man in the movie said, resistance is futile."

"Resistance isn't futile. I cannot succumb to the whirlpool if I want my career. Tonight, you can make up for it – and for calling me names – by giving me a ride to the shop. I've got a party to go to."

Nineteen

Sleep had just come and he had that wonderful feeling of respite after a long work day that had stretched itself well into the night. He'd taken one of the empty duty rooms – something he did occasionally. He'd slept in so many over the years, they seemed like old friends. And, it eliminated the twenty extra minutes it would take to drive each way – tonight, and again in the morning. His relaxation and trip to slumber land was broken by the buzzing of his phone.

"Son of a –," he started as he struggled out of his relaxed state, enmity building against whoever was pulling him out tonight. "If this is some idiot's idea of a joke –" He grabbed the phone and almost dropped it. He looked at the calling number; it was the lieutenant's. "This better not be a spider in the kitchen or a damn squirrel in the attic." He punched the button to answer, "Jackson," he growled. There was no immediate answer. *Jesus! A butt dial.* "Hello!" he said with more force. "Lieutenant!?"

Quietly he heard, "Chief?"

"Lieutenant? What's going on?"

Again, very quietly and slowly, "Help. Please."

Anger disappeared. His stomach dropped, and he was suddenly cold. "Where are you?"

Nothing.

"Lieutenant! Where are you?"

"Car."

"Are you hurt? Are you hurt!?"

"Weak. Sleepy."

"Have you been in a wreck?"

Nothing.

"Lieutenant! Have you been in a wreck?"

"Stopped."

"Where? Where!?"

"Road."

"Which road? Lieutenant!"

Nothing.

"Shit!" He grabbed the land line next to the bed and dialed the mobile number of the station's corpsman, Angela Jones.

She answered on the third ring. "This better not be for some come-as-you-are party."

"Jonesy, the lieutenant called. We've got a problem. She's out somewhere in her vehicle and sounded hurt – or weak – when she called. I need to find her and need you in case she's hurt. How soon can you get here?"

"If I can get there in less than twenty minutes, can I have a 72-hour pass?"

"I'll make it a 96."

"Cool."

Two minutes later, just as he was buttoning his shirt, there was a knock on his door. When he opened it, a thin African American woman, Angela Jones, was standing there in civilian clothes.

"How the hell –,"

"I decided to stay over and was sleeping next door."

"Cute."

"Hey, I made an offer. You countered and I accepted. Just good business."

"Okay, let's go."

They double-timed out of the building and to the chief's spot. Parked there was his 1940 Ford pickup truck.

"Do better in mine," said Angela. "It was made in this century."

"This will be okay," he replied. They jumped into the truck, and it started with a growl. He backed out of the spot and took off like a shot. Tires dug into the pavement then squealed as the truck accelerated. Bright head lights illuminated the road. The ride was smooth.

"I guess you've been working on this."

"Yeah," he said absentmindedly. He was focused on finding the lieutenant. "Any ideas where she might be?"

"There was some sort of dinner – or party – or something at the club tonight. Heard her and Annie talking when they left."

"That's thirty miles!" He thought for a moment, then, "Okay, we'll head for the club. If we don't see her along the way, we'll backtrack to the road where she'd turn off to drive home. And hope."

"You're going to a lot of trouble. Why not call 911? Why didn't she?"

"I don't know why she didn't. I didn't – in part – because I don't know where she is."

"In part? What's the other part?"

"Something I want to know before I turned her over to the official system."

"Like?"

"I don't know what's going on. Until I do, I don't want any unnecessary attention."

The truck was flying, the speedometer at 95. The roadside scenery shot by in a blur. He slowed to 60 when they passed the turnoff to her apartment complex. He looked up the road, but seeing nothing, he continued toward the club, still twenty miles away.

"Scan the sides. I don't want to miss her."

"Well," she replied, "you keep your eyes on the road. I don't mind helping out, but I don't particularly want to die tonight."

"You'll be – there. There on the left. The silver SUV."

"Leave it to Snow White –"

He glared at her.

"I mean the lieutenant, to drive one of those piddly little SUVs. Hate those things."

The truck skidded to a halt in the gravel, off the road, about ten feet from the SUV they'd spotted.

"Let's hope were not about to break up some teenager's love session," she said.

They ran to the vehicle; he beat Angela by a wide margin. Slumped in the driver's seat was Dee Cruise, apparently unconscious. The door was slightly ajar, as if she'd opened it in an attempt to get out.

"Lieutenant." No response. "Lieutenant!"

There was a slight wrinkling around her eyes, like she was listening, but in a dream.

"Take a quick look, Jonesy. Let me know what you think."

The corpsman opened her bag and removed a couple of items. "What I think is that I shouldn't have answered my phone." She began a quick assessment. After about 5 minutes, she turned and said, "I should do some other tests, but unless she gets worse, I think she should be able to sleep this off."

"Drunk?"

"Let's get her back to the station. Unless you want to do the rational thing and either call an ambulance or take her to the ER."

"Help me get her into the passenger seat. Then, you can drive her to the station and I'll meet you there."

"Uh, I'll help get her into the passenger side, but I can't drive an automatic. I'll have to drive the truck."

"What! You can't drive an automatic? But you can drive a stick?"

"Hey. You want to dance with the devil, there are consequences – payments, bribes, you know."

"I'm beginning to wish you hadn't answered your phone either," but he didn't mean it.

They moved Dee to the passenger seat and belted her in. She was lighter than he'd expected. He threw Jonesy the keys and said, "You hurt that truck and you'll be dancing with the devil yourself – tonight – in person."

"Trust me. I'll baby it all the way back."

He checked to make sure Dee's belt was tight and as he started the SUV, the roar of an engine and the sound of his truck tires squealing down the road filled the empty night. He shook his head.

Back at the station, he carried her from her vehicle to the bunk room in her office.

He looked at Jonesy and said, "Can you get her out of her uniform and into something else?"

"Shouldn't be a problem. Don't want to go through her things. You got a t-shirt and maybe running shorts I could use? She's probably going to swim in them, but it'll be better than her uniform. Oh, yeah, try to get me some that aren't stenciled. Something happens and we end up in the ER, it won't look good to have your name stenciled on the stuff she's wearing."

He returned in five minutes with shorts and a t-shirt.

"Now, leave me alone. I'm going to get her changed and do a couple more tests."

Twenty minutes later, Jonesy emerged from her room. "Damn, chief, you look like hell. Why you so worried about her?"

"She's new. She's nice." *She proved herself to me.* "I think she could do good here. I'd like to find out what happened before we do something that could hurt or end her career. What do you think? Too much to drink?"

"No. Not enough alcohol on her breath. I took some blood. I'll be surprised if she's even close to the legal limit."

"Drugs?!"

"Just because I'm African American and come from the inner-city, people think I know all about drugs. Stereotyping, that's what it is. I should be offended."

"Sorry."

"Yeah, well, I kinda do. And it is drugs. Maybe not what you think."

"Over the counter stuff? Please don't tell me you think she's got a drug problem."

"Snow White? No. I know all the signs. She doesn't have THAT kind of a drug problem."

"What the hell are you saying?"

"Unless I miss my guess, somebody roofied her ass."

"Somebody what?"

"Somebody slipped a date rape drug into her drink. Maybe Rohypnol. Actually, illegal in this country."

"You mean —"

"Yeah, unless the bartender is randomly slipping stuff into drinks, some fine and upstanding officer in the United States Coast Guard got ahold of an illegal drug and dosed your lieutenant in an attempt to rape her later — and keep her from remembering."

He slumped back in his chair. "Holy shit."

"Yeah. Holy shit. Anyway, I got blood and urine. I'll run it to the lab — a friend will run it on the QT. Then, we'll know for sure."

"Run it as a medical specimen for now, okay Jonesy? Not legal. Just in case it comes back different. I don't want it to be used against her. Not 'til we find out what happened. I'll sit with her."

Petty Officer Jones left the room, then returned a minute later without the specimens. She poured herself a cup of coffee and took a couple of sips. Then, she retrieved the specimens from the other room. "There, that breaks the chain of custody. Can't be used for legal now." She left the room.

Crap, he thought. *All I wanted was a quiet night's sleep. And now this. Roofies. And officers.*

Twenty

Dee Cruise sat on the side of her bunk in her duty room. She had a cup of strong tea in her hands and was sipping it. Her head was foggy and she wanted to lie back down.

"God, I feel terrible. I don't even know how I got here."

"Can you tell me what you remember about last night?" Scott asked. He was seated on a chair. Petty Officer Jones was leaning against the door jam.

"Last night?"

"Yeah. Please." He thought she was struggling with the concept of 'last night."

"There was a dinner at the club. It was supposed to be sort of a hail and farewell — you know for new people coming in and those transferring out."

He was familiar with hail and farewell parties.

"Anyway," she took another sip of the tea, "there weren't very many people there. Maybe a dozen or so."

"Can you remember who they were?"

She rattled off the names of four female officers and a couple of males. "I don't really remember everyone I met. I remember the women wanted to form a group, you know, get together on a regular basis. A couple of the men seemed interested, if you know what I mean. Not in the women's group – in the women."

Jackson looked at Jones who mouthed the words Snow White and rolled her eyes. Dee was shy, innocent, or naïve. Any way you cut it, she wasn't the type to be living on the 'wild side.'

"Please, go on."

"The whole thing started late, about 8 PM. I figured it was Friday night, so I could at least sleep in on Saturday – uh, today. Is it Saturday? We had a drink – champagne. I sipped mine, I didn't want to get loaded at my first function here and make a fool of myself or get busted for DUI on the way home. Dinner was served about 9. Captain Trahir showed up about 8:30. There were speeches and jokes. The dinner took about two hours. Afterward, most went into the lounge and were going to have a night cap. I'd only had one glass of wine with dinner, so I figured I could have one more. I wasn't feeling anything. I went to the ladies' room and when I returned, there was a glass of red wine on the table in front of my seat."

"So, you don't have any idea who bought it?"

"No. I was drinking it slowly and got less than half way through it when I started to feel kind of woozy. I figured I should get out of there, so I said a quick goodbye and left. I was starting to have a little bit of trouble walking and seeing, but it wasn't terrible."

"Anybody say anything?"

"One of the women asked if I was okay. I said yes. Two of the men, a lieutenant and a lieutenant commander, both asked if I was okay."

"And that's it?"

"Yes. Wait, I remember that just as I was leaving, Captain Trahir asked me too. He said he could call a taxi or get me a ride home."

Scott Jackson sat and thought for a moment.

"Okay, so you left the club and then what?"

"I don't know how far I got, but I knew my vision and coordination were going fast. I didn't drink that much. I don't understand." She paused, stared, shook her head and sipped her tea. "I'm not sure what after that. I think I remember calling someone."

"Me."

"You?"

"Yup."

"I'm sorry. I didn't know who —"

"Well, better me than someone you didn't know."

"I'm sorry. I didn't mean to get that drunk. I didn't think I was."

"You weren't." It was Petty Officer Jones.

"What?"

"Somebody roofied your a —" a quick look from the chief stopped her in mid-sentence. "I mean, somebody put rohypnol into that last glass of wine. If it had been sooner, you'd been asleep in your dessert."

"Rohypnol?"

"Other countries use it as a sedative. It's illegal here. Mostly used as a date rape drug."

"A – date – rape – drug?" She struggled with the idea that someone at the club would do such a thing. No. That can't be. I was at the club – with other officers." Dee began to look around the room, then started to try to cover up more. She looked very vulnerable and afraid.

"You're safe here," he said.

Of course she was safe here. But she'd thought she was safe at the club, too.

"It would appear that one of your colleagues meant to rape you and not have you remember," he continued.

Dee sat. Stunned. She stared straight ahead. When he spoke again, she jumped.

"Petty officer Jones had a friend run some lab tests – after we got back. Negligible alcohol, but there was the rohypnol. I've called the investigators. They're going to take your statement. You can't talk to anyone who was there last night. Understand?"

She stared at him in disbelief.

Later that afternoon, the investigator arrived and took Dee's statement.

"That looks good. You've actually done better than other victims," she said.

"Other victims?" *How many?* Thoughts wouldn't come. *The club should be safe. They are – they are – officers.*

"We're making progress. We don't want anyone who was there to have any idea there was an attempt. Even those you believe above suspicion. Let me know if anyone calls you checking on how you are or if you had any problem getting home," she said, handing Dee a business card. "Oh, I wouldn't let anyone buy you a drink without watching as it is made, poured, or opened."

As the investigator left, Dee said, half under her breath, "What is happening to the world?"

There was a knock on the door. It was the Scott with a mug of tea. "How you doing?"

"I'm not sure anymore. I mean, the world seems to have turned upside down." Suddenly, she was aware that she was wearing only a t-shirt and running shorts, supplied by him. She blushed slightly, embarrassed and said, "I should get into something more appropriate." She wanted to cover up, to hide.

"Uh, yeah. When we got you back here, we didn't want to go through your things, so Jonesy got you out of your things and into these," he gestured at the shirt and shorts and tried to focus on other parts of the room.

"Well, thank you for everything you did. I'm really sorry if –" Then, "I'll make sure to launder these before I return them."

"I'm glad you called – if you can't count on us –," he said. "There's no need to wash those. I can just –"

"No, really, it's no problem."

Both blushed, and Jackson turned and left, pausing in the doorway, turning halfway back, as if he wanted to say something more.

Twenty-one

Scott Jackson absentmindedly looked through some paperwork as he mulled over the events of the last — he looked at his watch — fourteen hours. Had it only been fourteen hours?

She'd called him. Not the police or 911. Him. Why? And he went looking for her by himself, well, along with Jonesy. He knew why he'd taken Jonesy. If there had been a wreck. If she'd been hurt.

When he'd seen her vehicle — when it didn't look like it had rolled, or had crashed, he'd been relieved. *After all, I didn't want the OIC to be hurt. Was that it?* Finding her practically unconscious worried him. So, they'd brought her back here — partly because Jonesy said she'd be able to sleep it off. He was amazed at how little she seemed to weigh when he carried her to the passenger side of her car. She was the lieutenant, but at that time, she was tiny, vulnerable, and in need of protection.

Once they were back here, he'd worried over her like a mother hen. Sure, he would have been in trouble if she'd gone south and he'd had to explain himself, but he knew in the back of his mind there was more to it than that. It was more than she was one of 'his responsibilities.' He wanted to put his hands over his ears and yell, 'Shut up! Shut up! Shut up!"

Then, this morning, when she seemed to be okay, when he'd brought her tea, she seemed so delicate, vulnerable. He wanted to protect her. He tried not to stare at her legs, sticking out from his running shorts. The image of her legs burned in his mind. Soft, and at the same time, strong. Perfect light skin on perfectly shaped legs. *I hope Jonesy didn't seen me staring.*

He shook his head in an effort to clear the image. While it wasn't lust, there was caring, attraction. It had been a long time. It was that word that he refused to accept that was hiding out somewhere in his brain. Not since –

When they told her about the rohypnol, she'd looked even more vulnerable. She'd tried to cover up more, as if covering herself with a thin sheet would keep her safer. He could try to imagine what she felt, but he knew it would be fruitless. She'd been preyed upon and probably escaped rape, maybe worse, by a narrow margin. It would destroy any sense of security she had. Anger boiled. Anger at the monster who would think this was acceptable. Life would not be normal – not even after they caught this bastard – not for a long time.

His thoughts were broken by a cough behind him. When he turned, he saw her standing there, in the door. She was in uniform, with the shorts and t-shirt in her hand.

"I didn't want to bother you; I wanted to thank you again. I'm headed out – for my apartment." Her eyes drifted as she spoke, as if apologetic.

"Look, lieutenant –"

"As long as there aren't any others around – to think it is a sign of disrespect for an officer – please call me Dee. You've earned that more than my fellow officers –"

"Ma'am, uh, Dee. It may or may not have been one of your fellow officers. And you're one of us – at this station. We'll do whatever we can to safeguard our own."

"Well, thank you for that – Scott. If I may?"

"Certainly, ma'am, uh Dee. This isn't as easy as you might think. And you don't have to do the t-shirt and shorts."

"I insist. It's really the least I can do. Thank you, again." She turned and walked away.

He watched her go. He would have taken the t-shirt and shorts. Truth be told, he wanted to have something with her scent on it. He asked himself why – then blushed slightly, knowing he wanted something that had been so close to her – and maybe give him the feeling of being closer to her, too.

Twenty-two

"So, what you're saying is that some officer at the club slipped something into your drink?" asked Annie. It was Monday morning.

"That's pretty much the way it looks."

"And, no idea who?"

"No."

"God, that's creepy. Makes me want to look over my shoulder," said Annie.

"Makes you want to look over *YOUR* shoulder. I'm not sure if I'm paranoid or if paranoid isn't enough."

"Yeah. I'd probably go with the second. So, what happened?"

"I started feeling woozy. After dinner. There was a glass of wine at my place – I found it when I returned from the ladies' room. I thought somebody was just being nice."

"I'll check that off my list. Any drinks delivered unknown can go into the sink."

"Yeah. I thought it was just hitting me – you know, the alcohol. So, I decided to get home before I got too drunk to drive. But as I headed down the road, I felt like I was getting really drunk really fast. I was able to pull off the road. That's pretty much all I remember. Except before I passed out, I called Scott."

Annie was silent. Then, "Not to make light of what happened to you, but when did Chief Jackson become Scott?"

Dee turned her head. "What? Well, that's his name. I called him and he – along with Petty Officer Jones, found me and brought me back here." Her face was getting warm. *Dammit!*

"No. No. You've made a transition. He was Chief Petty Officer Jackson. Now, he's Scott. And, you called him. Not 911. Not me. Scott. Why him? And while we're at it, I wonder why he brought you back here instead of either calling an ambulance or taking you to the hospital." She sat back, a smug look on her face.

"Who do you think you are, the DA? I don't know why I called him. I did. I hit a button on my phone. And, I just referred to him as Scott. Big deal. You're making more out of this than you should."

"Am I? First, the change from chief to Scott indicates a change in your relationship, at least inside you. A closer feeling, recognition of –"

"You're being ridiculous," but she could feel the growing heat in her face.

"And, when you thought you were in trouble –"

"I was in trouble," she said it quietly, acknowledging, maybe for the first time to herself, that she had been in dire straits.

"When you were in trouble, something *inside you* reached out to him."

Dee looked at Annie.

"I should be enjoying this more than I am," Annie continued. "I was hoping to lighten the mood. That didn't work, but don't think you're off the hook. That instant sunburn when I pointed out you referred to him as Scott – it's like an admission that it wasn't just a slip of the tongue."

There was a knock on the door. Both women jumped slightly. Scott entered the office with a folder.

"I thought you might want to see the call log for this week – ma'am. This is a copy for your files."

She took the folder. "Yes, thank you."

He left the office, closing the door behind him.

"And, he's hovering," said Annie. "The 'ma'am' was a bit delayed. Did he just add it for my benefit?"

"No. He's being proper. As he should be. But he has asked me to call the duty petty officer every night and report when I'm in quarters – a way to make sure I'm home safe. I told him it's silly, but he was fairly insistent. Even quoted some regulation. Probably BS."

"And if you don't report?"

"I didn't ask. I assume someone will come looking."

"Someone? God! You ARE naïve."

Twenty-three

Dee sat in her office trying to concentrate on her work. Her mind wouldn't focus on the tasks at hand. *Okay. Somebody tried to set me up for rape. And what else? Certainly, if they thought they could get away with rape, they wouldn't consider –* She shivered. *What else would they do? Could she have gotten the wrong drink? Maybe it was all a mistake. Yes. A mistake. It must have been a mistake. Who would want to – I don't really know anyone here. Why would someone pick me? But, even if it wasn't me, that doesn't make it any better. It means somebody else was meant to be raped. And – and what?*

She kept running the possibilities through her mind. It all came back to her. The drink was at her place – anonymously. Nobody knew who put it there. So, whoever did, must have been after someone in her group. But everyone else was already seated. Or were they? How could somebody have put a glass in her place unseen if everyone else had already been seated? Someone who nobody else noticed? A member of the group, or a member of the wait staff. It kept coming back to her, and it made her feel more and more afraid. Some unknown person – well, and unknown person on a list of about twelve, counting the bartender and wait staff, was out to drug her.

She sat back in her chair, staring at the ceiling. Her mind refused to clear.

There was a knock on the door. Her head snapped down. It turned out to be the chief – Scott. She motioned for him to enter.

"Good morning. I wanted to check and see how you are doing."

"I'm okay."

"You sure? You seem distracted."

"Okay. I'm not okay. I keep trying to tell myself that the drink – and everything that was intended afterward – was intended for someone else. That doesn't make it any better, and to tell the truth, I think it had to be intended for me. That means that there is someone out there who has targeted me for –"

"Yes, ma'am. I've come to the same conclusion. I'm hoping that Agent Harvard will get a lead or two and nail this son of a – sorry ma'am. Just the way I feel about someone – some monster who would do a thing like this."

"Well, thank you. It's nice – comforting to know I have people looking out for me. If I were totally alone it would be much harder." *You know, that's really true.*

"You do have people who care about you and want to make sure you are safe. Why don't we get you out of the office for a few hours? I have to do some welfare checks. They're easy, and if you come along, it might get your mind off all this," he gestured to the paperwork languishing on her desk, "and give you a few hours of respite."

"Welfare checks?"

"Yeah. Fishermen. We go out and check to make sure they have licenses, registrations, safety equipment. Nice day to be on the water, and this gives us an excuse. I think you'll enjoy the break. Besides, we've got a big inspection coming up, and if you come along, we've got one more person to help with the preparation for that."

"Well, I'm not doing much good here. I might as well tag along. I can put it down to seeing what my people do out on the water."

"Good idea, ma'am. I'll see you down by the pier in twenty minutes."

Twenty-four

The response boat left the small harbor and headed out to sea – southwest, then south by south west – to check on fishermen. The sun was behind them in a bright blue sky. The waves were small and the water a deep blue. Dee looked at Scott sitting in the right seat. He was looking out on the water – not searching, he just seemed to be taking it in.

"Penny for your thoughts."

"Huh?" He turned and looked at her. "Oh, sometimes I just like to watch the ocean. A couple more miles out, if we stop, or slow, you'll see the deepest blue you've ever seen. And the way the water moves, every second the surface changes." His hand was in the air, moving like the water. "It's a dynamic work of art. Most folks don't get it. They say something like, 'Yeah. Water moves.' But it's more than that. It's mesmerizing."

"You sound more like a philosopher or artist than a chief."

"Who's to say you can't be both?"

"Well, no one, I guess. Mind if I ask you a question?"

"You mean two questions. You just asked me one."

"Oh, my god!" She opened her eyes wide and sagged a bit in faux astonishment. "We're back to philosopher and I'm not sure I'm ready for that."

"Your second question?" he asked, smiling.

"Why the Coast Guard?"

"My family has a tradition. Family are expected to spend a career in the service of the country. Some go to various branches of the military. I thought the Coast Guard would give me a chance to serve, see a little action, and not travel to weird places in the world."

"You don't like to travel?" Her brow wrinkled as she asked.

"I love to travel. I'm just not hot on going to some far-off place where those indigenous to the place hate us and want to kill us. Besides, we've got enough of our own problems to deal with. I figured I could help on the home front."

"And, you're expected to spend a career? What if you wanted to do something else? Like philosophy, or art. You will have spent your life doing – well, not to belittle it – this, instead."

He was laughing. "I have got a degree in philosophy. Not that you can do much in the real world with that. But I wanted a degree in philosophy. This gives me a chance to have that degree and actually do something useful in the real world. Not many companies out there with jobs for philosophers. And, I've had a LOT of fun doing what I'm doing. I may not have changed the world, but I think I've made my little part better. Better than if I had become an investment banker, or real estate tycoon. I've saved people who would have died. I've stopped a fair share of drugs and human trafficking. Even been in a few shoot outs. Where else can you do that? Besides, I haven't spent my life. I can retire – soon – at 37."

"Yeah. Your record is great. So, you chose to stay here. Not that I'm saying that's wrong, but –"

"Yes, and I could have fought my way up the ladder. To do that, I'd be stationed in some big facility, but like I said earlier, probably playing with paperwork all day. Overweight and out of shape. No thanks. This may end up being my sunset tour, but it's in a great place with great people. I'm having fun and I've got more freedom here. I can make a difference in my troopers' lives and careers."

"So, what after this?" *I hope that 'sunset' is a few years off.*

"Me first. Why did you choose the Coast Guard? You're smart. A college grad. You could have done something else. Why this?"

Yes. Why this? Should I tell him the truth? "I was in school. Senior year – well, the start of it. I saw a poster. I was considering all of the services, but the Coast Guard seemed to give me a little more control over where I was going to go and what I was going to do. Plus, as we talked, they said they'd pay for my senior year – and a Master's later on." *And it got me the hell away from –*

"So, why here? You're a long way from Cape May and the big time. This posting might not improve your chances for promotion – I assume that's important."

"Actually, your friend, George Pierce. He saw me bored with carrying papers around – as you say – and suggested that an operational tour would be one way to distinguish myself in my career. Yes, promotion and success are very important to me. He actually brought me the announcement that this particular position would be opening up and said it was the right one for me. A good start. And, if that wasn't enough, he said you would be a great teacher to help me do the things I'd need to do to get – as he put it, a leg up." After a minute, "I hope that didn't make you head swell inside your helmet." She smiled.

"George's a good guy. From time to time, we've helped each other with 'problem children,'" he paused.

Her heart sunk. She stared at the console. "I –"

"Or with somebody each felt had great potential and deserved any benefit we might bring. A small station like this is the perfect place to learn more in a year than you would learn in ten years in a monolithic but sterile environment."

She turned toward the window. When she looked back, he was staring out the opposite window.

"You could have finished that thought a little more quickly. You had me thinking I was one of your 'problem children,' as you put it."

"Sorry. I didn't want to cause you any pain when your head swelled inside your helmet." He was laughing, and now, so was she.

"By the way," he added. "The fishing story."

"Yes. The fishing story. Your response was really strange. What's the deal?"

"George was sending me a message. It took me a little while."

"What kind of message? And why couldn't he just call? How would he know I would pass it along?"

"Wow! Twenty questions. He made it important enough that you'd remember. He could have called, but he wanted to be cute. He's like that."

"So, what's the message?"

"He was telling me what you are like. A marlin is a strong, independent fish. Fun to catch. Don't take the analogy too far. He was telling me that you're a good person – who can be trusted."

"Trusted?"

"Yeah. There are officers who can be trusted and those – let's just say those with whom we are strictly by the book. So, if you couldn't be trusted, he would have you tell me about the time we went camping and I ended up with a snake in my tent. If you were okay, but a dud, it might have been boar hunting. He likes to have me figure these things out."

"So – I'm not sure I even know what to ask."

"So, he was telling me you are worth any extra effort you might need to help your career, that you will be a strong and independent leader – and you'd probably be okay with some of our 'alternate ways' of doing things."

"Alternate ways?"

"Not illegal, just creative. It makes things easier for us – and ultimately, for you. Officers almost always do things just by the book. Enlisted find back channels. End arounds. Not illegal, although they can be questionable at times. Things get done. Sometimes it's best not to ask how." Then, "That looks like a group of fishing boats. I would recommend we start there – ma'am."

Twenty-five

They started with a twenty-five-foot Blackfin, a boat with an open deck and small cabin with large windows. Three men were on board. They hailed the boat and came alongside. Scott crossed onto the boat and chatted with the men. He looked at their safety gear, including life jackets, and checked to see each person had a fishing license. Then he returned to the response boat.

"We aren't required to check fishing licenses," she said.

"No. You're right, but as long as we're out here, we might as well. Gives Fish and Game a hand. Mostly, we're checking safety equipment, registrations, that sort of thing – kind of as a way to make sure they aren't smuggling or running drugs or people." He settled himself in his seat and fastened his restraints.

"How do you do that?"

"Mostly, they give themselves away. People who are doing things right and lawfully are usually friendly and interested in chatting. Especially if you happen to know where the fish are biting. And, they're usually happy to show you what they've caught, or complain about what they haven't caught. When people start to look nervous, that's when we want to check more closely."

"Shouldn't we have brought another body? Maybe be ready for trouble?"

"If we run across anything suspicious today, we'll just back off and call for reinforcements. We won't take any chances. We're a little shorthanded today with the quarterly inspection coming up, and I want to be sure everything is ready for that. If we fail the inspection, it means working weekends – everybody – until we can pass the second one – which is usually done pretty strictly. I haven't had any issues here. Mostly people out for a day's fishing – and beering."

They pulled away from that boat and headed for the next. It also held three men. They looked to be in their forties and had lines in the water.

"What you catching?" asked Scott.

"Not much of anything. Not that we really want to catch much of anything," one of the men laughed as he took a pull from his beer. "Mostly, we come out here to sit around and have a few beers."

"And get away from the 'honey-do' lists," laughed a second man. "Nice to have some peace and quiet. Wives don't believe we can get any messages out here, and the radio doesn't work."

"Your radio doesn't work?" asked Scott.

"Might if I turn it on," and all the men laughed.

Scott just shook his head. "Life jackets?"

There were four hanging near the entrance of the cabin. They also pointed out the fire extinguisher and showed him the boat registration.

Scott returned to the response boat. "Boys will be boys," he said, shaking his head. "From time immemorial, guys have tried to find ways to stay out when 'mom' wants them home."

They motored slowly away and to the next boat. The sun had passed its high point and was on the way down.

"There's a marina about twenty minutes from here. Why don't we head over there and grab a bite and do a comfort stop?" he said.

"Sounds good. I could use a little of both."

They motored to a small marina, Sandy's Shanty, in a small protected inlet. There was an area large enough to accommodate their boat along the side of the floating piers. In all, there was room for about ten boats on wooden floating fingers reaching into the small cove. They tied up and headed past the few picnic tables outside into the restaurant. They bought hamburgers and fries at the counter and headed outside to sit in the shade of a eucalyptus tree. A cool breeze blew through.

"This place is lovely," said Dee.

"I come here from time to time. The food is good and the people are nice," Scott said taking a sip of his coffee.

As he said it, two men waved from a boat pulling out.

"If I'd taken a billet at a large facility – to punch my ticket for promotion," he said as he waved back, "I wouldn't have days like this. I'd be eating my brown bag lunch while I was in some hastily called meeting about nothing important. I've got a lot of freedom here."

They sat in silence for a bit, eating slowly and enjoying the ocean breeze in the shade.

"I guess we should get back to it," he said finally. "Coffee to go?"

"Sure." She started to dig in her pocket.

"P-l-e-a-s-e," he said as he rolled his eyes.

"I should buy."

"You can buy next time," he said as he headed to the counter. He returned with two go cups.

As they walked back to the boat, she sipped hers. *Perfect. Two cream, half a Splenda.*

Twenty-six

They headed back out to an area just south of where they'd been before and spotted a 23-foot Stingray Sport Deck in the distance. There was no cover, and the bow in front of the windscreen contained enough seating for four friendly people. The boat was just drifting, and there were six people aboard. As they approached, they could see there were three males and three females, all appeared to be in their early twenties.

"Howdy folks."

"Uh is there a problem, officer?"

"It's chief. I'm in the Coast Guard. We're just checking to make sure you have your safety gear and if there are any problems."

"Un, no problems here, offi – excuse me, chief."

"Good. Who's driving?"

"I am." He was a good sized, sun-bleached blond male, wearing swim trunks and a tank top. His tan showed he'd spent many days and hours in the sun.

"May I see some identification and the registration, please?"

Reluctantly, he reached into a cabinet and pulled out his wallet and identification, also the registration. He handed his ID to Scott.

"Registration shows it is owned by William Jefferson. And this is Lance."

Scott returned the ID and registration. "Life jackets?"

"Under the seats."

"Please."

They lifted the seats, and there were six life jackets. "Thank you. Please make sure everybody knows how to put one on. Thank you, and have a nice day."

Scott returned to the response boat. Just before they pulled away, he heard one of the males say, "Hey, that chic was hot. Maybe I should join the Coast Guard." The males laughed. The females just looked put out.

Dee backed away from the boat, turned, and accelerated slowly.

"Hey," he said, "you're a chic."

"At least I'm hot."

"Yeah, and unless I miss my guess, you're going to have some twenty-year-old chasing after you." He was laughing.

"Laugh all you want. When I'm ninety, he'll only be eighty." Then, they were both laughing. "Besides, you're just jealous – none of the ladies said anything about you being hot."

"Yeah, that's what I need, a girl young enough to get me thrown in jail thinking I'm hot. Women are smarter than that."

She unstrapped her helmet and took it off, setting it on the seat behind her. She flipped her head and ran her fingers through her hair.

"I don't know. Sometimes both men and women want a fling. When it's done, it's done. You have to find a good way to end it. Sometimes it's hard, but if you do it, you need to make it quick and final."

Scott was quiet. When she looked at him, he was looking out the side window. From what she could see, his face was hard.

"Sorry. If you'll tell me what it was, I'll apologize and promise not to say it again."

She got no response for a minute, then, "It was a long time ago. I should have gotten over it, but I guess I haven't. You couldn't have known. No apology necessary."

After a pause, she decided to change the conversation, "So, what do you think about them?"

"Lance definitely wants to be BMOC – Big Man on Campus – and he's taking friends out on daddy's boat. They're going to get drunk and probably smoke some weed. Then, most of them will be puking over the side. I just hope that somebody is sober enough to make sure those who are puking don't fall overboard."

Dee turned the boat and started to head for home.

"Why don't we just head north," said Scott. "We can wait out here until the sun goes down then see if you can find your way back in the dark."

He seemed to be back in normal spirits, and she was happy to be out here with him a little longer. *I am going to have a sit-down with Annie and see if we can figure out what set him off earlier.* She pointed the boat north and set off at a slow cruise.

Twenty-seven

The response boat moved along slowly in the waning day. The swells were beginning to dampen as the sun touched the horizon. Pastel clouds hung low.

"This is beautiful," she said.

"Yes, it's like this a lot. Same thing in the morning, if you're out far enough. My favorite time of day."

"You *are* an artist."

"Can't paint or draw to save my life."

"The artist is in the heart and soul, not in the ability."

"There's a boat out there," he pointed to a large cabin cruiser about a half mile further out. "Let's take a look."

She increased the speed a bit and headed for the boat.

"Fishing poles hanging off the stern." Then, almost to himself, "Kinda deep to be fishing here."

They pulled within a quarter mile. A woman was laying on the bow, apparently catching the last rays of the sun. A man in the cockpit was waving one hand in a friendly manner.

"Looks like they are doing fine," she said.

"Yeah. Doesn't hurt to check, though."

They got to within about sixty yards and Scott yelled, "Hard right! Hard right! Full power!"

"Huh?" She looked at him.

His eyes were wide open. He looked at her briefly then grabbed the helm and moved it hard to the right. A whoosh went close overhead. He pushed the throttle to its stops. The boat rolled hard and accelerated. Pinging sounds were coming rapidly from the side of the boat nearest the cabin cruiser. The windows were shattering. Glass shards were flying through the interior of the boat.

"We gotta get outa here!" he yelled.

The boat was slowing. Black smoke was billowing into the cabin. Grinding sounds were coming from one of the motors. Water was starting to fill the inside. Cold water. The sounds of gunfire and occasional pinging of bullets hitting the boat continued.

The black smoke grew more dense. The second motor made an unnatural sound. Then there was only quiet. And an occasional gunshot. He hoped they were bad shots and that their goal was to escape, not come after them and make sure they were dead.

Water continued to rise. He reached for the radio, then saw it was in pieces, hit by more than one bullet. He looked at her. She was slumped in her seat.

"Lieutenant! Lieutenant!" There was no response. "God – please, no."

He grabbed her wrist and tried to take her pulse, but his own heart was hammering away and taking a pulse was out of the question. He pulled back her life jacket and collar and looked at her neck. Everything was taking too long. *Come on. Come on.* Then, finally, he could see the artery in her neck pulsing. He rolled his eyes up. *Thank you.*

He hit his harness release, then hers. The water was now almost to his knees. He just had to pull her out of her seat and out the back of the cabin. Before the boat went to the bottom. He slid out of his seat and started to pull her. But she wouldn't budge. *God! Now What?* He pulled again. Same result, although the water was now above his knees. *Her foot's stuck!* He dove forward into the water, trying to feel where she was caught. His life jacket prevented him from getting deep enough to find out.

He came up for air and fumbled with the life jacket buckle. His hands were cold and he couldn't make them work fast enough. Finally, the preserver parted and he yanked it off, water now at his waist and up to her chest. He dove back down, now hunting in the dark. He felt her knee and worked his way down.

When he got to her ankle, he felt part of the panel that was in front of the seats. It had somehow come loose and was trapping her. He moved his hand under the metal and around her foot. Everything seemed to be intact, but he knew he had little time. He turned her foot inward and by pulling, then flexing her leg, he was able to free her foot. His lungs burning, he broke the surface and gasped for air. The water was now at her chin and rising. He pulled. Her harness was still holding her. He was ripping at it, trying to pull it free. It wasn't working. He pulled out his folding knife, flipped it open and started slashing at the harness furiously.

The bow was under water. The boat turned vertically, and started its slide beneath the waves. *No. No. No. No.* But the sea would not be denied, and the boat slid quickly. Scott gave one more pull, and she was free. They didn't escape as much as the boat sank from underneath them and the cabin door slid past. He watched the boat as it moved into the inky blackness of the ocean and disappeared.

He was breathing hard, and his heart was hammering in his chest. He had her by the life vest. She was still unconscious, but she was alive. And he hadn't allowed her to be pulled down with the ship. But they were adrift in the ocean, with full night only minutes away.

He looked around and saw his life jacket about ten yards away. He was about to take a chance and leave her where she was when he swam to retrieve it when the ocean boiled. He jumped, then realized the last of the air in their craft had escaped in one whoosh. He waited for a minute to settle down then towed her when he swam to his life jacket and put it on.

The ocean was calm. Small waves lifted and dropped them. His arm burned. He discovered he'd had a number of minor wounds. Most, he assumed, were from glass and metal fragments when the boat had been shot up. He knew the whoosh was probably a rocket propelled grenade. That meant drug runners. And that was bad news. More bad news. He was bleeding. She wasn't, as far as he could tell. But out here, in the dark water wasn't going to be the place to find out. He knew something would find out. There were sharks out here, and they could detect blood – very little blood – a long way off. He'd have to figure out something – and soon. Chances of them being found out here adrift were slim. And they wouldn't survive in the water. If the sharks didn't get them, the cold would. Then, all the sea creatures. He didn't relish becoming fish waste – alive or dead.

Out across the water in the light of a quarter moon, he saw the cabin cruiser. There were no lights and no sound. *Did they have another boat? Maybe they're gone. Doesn't seem like they'd be that quiet. Maybe they think we're dead.* He reasoned he had few options. Good or bad, the boat was the only choice. He took a breath and slowly, quietly, began a swim to the boat, pulling her along.

Twenty-eight

They'd been able to motor about a hundred yards away from the cabin cruiser before their little boat sank. The swim took longer than he would have thought, but then, he was towing her as well.

His arms were aching and he was breathing hard as he approached within ten yards. He decided to wait for a few minutes to determine if their attackers were still on board as well as to rest for the next part of his plan. They'd been a long way away when the boat went down. *Maybe that's why they didn't come after us. Maybe they thought we were dead – or they were just trying to escape. The boat's still there. Did they have another one?* He was aware of the unknown time limit – when the sharks would arrive.

He looked at the boat. He was wearing a side arm – a pistol. He didn't know if it would still work after being in the water for – how long had they been out here? The sun was down. A half-moon was up. He wondered if the water had gotten into the ammunition. If so, even if the gun worked, it would only click. Wet powder wouldn't work. He could try to bluff whoever it was with a nonfunctional gun, but why would a guy with a loaded assault rifle not shoot when facing a pistol?

After what he thought might be ten minutes, and sensing no life on the boat, he slowly approached the stern, keeping a hand on Dee, her face turned away so that her white skin wouldn't give them away in the moonlight if someone were still aboard. He kept his face mostly submerged for the same reason. With each stroke, he came closer and closer. With each stroke, he became more and more apprehensive.

He reached the swim platform on the stern of the boat and pulled her next to it. Keeping one hand on her, he lifted himself and crawled face first onto the platform from the waist up, then rolled to bring his legs onto it as well. Light tinkling, like from a wind chime, came from the cockpit. He froze and listened, but there was nothing else. He removed his life jacket and set it onto the platform, making as little noise as he could. Carefully, he raised his eyes just above the transom. In partial moonlight, he saw the empty cockpit and rifle casings rolling around on the deck. They were hitting each other and the sides. Occasionally, one would roll down the stairs and into the cabin. Every time one touched something, there was a small 'clink.'

He turned and sat on the swim platform, his legs dangling in the water. He pulled Dee and put her back against the platform. When the stern dipped into the waves with the rocking of the boat, he lifted her, still unconscious, into a sitting position on his lap. He rolled and placed her against the stern, then positioned her face up. He got to his knees and before heading over the transom to check the boat, he whispered in her ear, "Don't go anywhere. I'll be right back."

He slid over the transom on his stomach. There were casings everywhere – maybe two hundred. He slithered to the entrance of the cabin and lay there for a minute, listening for any noise. Nothing other than the clinking of the casings. He pulled out the pistol and his flip knife and said a quick prayer. *Maybe I can throw it, if nothing else,* he thought, looking at the pistol. The moon went behind a cloud, killing any light there might have been. *Here we go.*

He turned and slid down the stairs on his backside, one at a time, hugging the side of the stairwell, staying as small and quiet as possible and hoping to be able to face any danger immediately. He saw no one in the cabin. He worked his way forward and confirmed it. Breathing a sigh of relief and happy the cabin was empty, he turned to get Dee. There was a form tucked in the corner. He jumped and yelped in surprise. He pointed the pistol at the form. The form didn't move. His heart hammered in his chest.

He approached slowly. Still no movement. The moon came from behind the cloud, and he could see a man – he thought it was a man – naked from the waist up, but beaten brutally, to the point of disfigurement. There was a thin red gash across his throat. It didn't take and expert to tell he was dead.

He leaned against the far side of the boat for a minute to collect himself, then left the cabin, closing the door, and took in deep breaths. He checked to see that Dee was still secure on the swim platform, then moved around the cabin to the bow. The woman he'd seen earlier was still laying there. Her bikini was disheveled and there was a large red area on her forehead. She'd been shot. He hoped her fate was less brutal than the man below, although he knew it probably wasn't a quick end. A check of the bridge on the way back showed the radio had been smashed into pieces. *So much for radioing for help.*

Returning to the transom, he put his arms under Dee's and lifted her onto the transom then into the boat and carried her to a bench seat under cover in the cockpit, outside the cabin. He lay her on the cushion and returned to the cabin, finally finding two blankets forward. He took one and worked his way to the bow where he covered the dead woman, trying to be as careful as possible not to disturb any evidence.

There was no key in the ignition. He went to the engine compartment and opened it. All the ignition wires were missing. The engine wouldn't work. At least they were out of the water and had some cover.

Then, he returned to Dee. He removed her life jacket and tossed it onto the deck. He took a cushion from the opposite seat and crushed it into the corner. Then, shivering he sat in the corner against it and carefully pulled her against him, wrapping his legs and arms around her to keep them both warm. He pulled the blanket around them and rested his head against the cushion. His mind raced with the events of the day and things he needed to do. But foremost was the care and safety of the officer who lay against him wet, cold, and unconscious. Before long, the rocking of the waves and fatigue of his exertions, both physical and psychological, forced him into a deep sleep.

Twenty-nine

Dee Cruise was rocking back and forth on her grandparent's porch swing – relaxed and content. The sound of their wind chime comforting and relaxing. She was lying against soft pillows and engulfed in a comfortable warmth. All was right with the world. When she was a little girl and used to do this very same thing. Slowly she struggled. Somehow it couldn't be. Reality started to return.

She started to move her limbs. The rocking and clinking remained. Then, she remembered. *The boat. Gunfire. Then, what?* She opened her eyes. There was darkness. And the rocking. She was lying against – against, a body. Her body tightened. She looked up. It was Scott. She relaxed. *But where are we?* She moved slightly.

"Well, hello," he said, yawning. "I'm glad you woke up. How are you feeling?"

"Okay."

"I hope you don't mind. You were shivering and I wanted to be sure you weren't cold. I used the blanket and myself to keep you warm. I don't usually wrap myself around unconscious women."

"Uh, no. It's fine. I mean, thank you." *I wish I'd had more time to enjoy it.* What happened?" She started to sit up and felt a twinge of pain in her head. *Ow.*

"Easy, you've got a bump there. Apparently, you hit your head on the side when I flipped the boat around."

"I guess I missed all the action. What happened?"

"They shot up the boat. It sank. I was able to pull you out and swim over here. Happily, our friends bailed out, so I didn't have to fight my way aboard. Whoever owns the boat wasn't as lucky as we were. He's in the cabin. She's on the bow."

"I take it they are both dead."

"Yeah. Not pretty."

"Well, I need to use the – head – so I guess it is in the cabin."

"Yeah. You might want to avoid looking in the aft port corner when you come out. They did a real job on him."

"Sure. I should be okay."

She entered the cabin and went forward. The head was past the table and before the bedroom in the bow. She relieved herself and was returning to the cockpit when she looked at the dead man. Getting closer, she saw his face had practically been obliterated and bruises and cuts covered his naked torso. The gash on his throat went from ear to ear.

Her stomach tightened and she knew she was going to throw up. She rushed from the cabin and headed for the transom. Just before she reached it, she started retching violently. Almost nothing came out – she hadn't eaten in hours. Still, her body was trying to rid itself of anything left inside.

Scott was there in an instant. "Easy. Easy. You'll be okay. Easy." He held her hair and put his arm around her, keeping her from falling into the sea.

After what seemed an eternity, her retching slowed, then stopped. "I – uh – thought – I'd – seen –"

"Yeah. This one's bad."

"I can't imagine – was the woman –"

"One shot. Clean. That doesn't mean – anyway, the medical examiner will make the determination."

"What kind of people do this – I mean how could you –"

"In my experience, drug runners. These might have been their contacts, you know, the ones who take the drugs from the mother ship into port. Maybe they missed a payment – stole some drugs. Who knows? Penalties in that business are pretty nasty."

"You've seen this before?"

"Yeah. I used to do drug interdiction."

"How did you manage to –"

"I was young, and tough, or thought I was. Some lose it after they reach a certain age. I started to see all the negative things. Even stopping the drugs wasn't enough. So, I asked to be transferred and decided to leave the drug wars to others who still had the fire. I still wanted to see the drugs stopped, I just didn't seem to have –"

"I'm sorry." And she put her arms around him. After a minute she tasted the foulness in her mouth. "Now, I'm really sorry. I'm a mess and I've got to rinse my mouth." She started to get up.

"You sit. You've had a head injury. I'll go below and see if I can find some water." He disappeared below and returned a few minutes later with three bottles of water. "All with original seals. Should be okay."

She took one, opened it, listening for the seal to break. Then, she took a healthy mouthful, rinsed, and spit over the side. Two more times was enough to clear the foul taste.

"What about the woman. Do I need to look at her – you know, for the report?"

"No. She's dead alright. The medical examiner will determine cause, although I'd say that will be obvious." He looked around, then at his watch. "Sun will be coming up in a couple of hours. We should rest." A rain squall developed a short distance away and headed toward them. They headed back under cover of the cockpit and sat on the bench seat they'd occupied previously. She started to shiver and he wrapped the blanket around them as best he could. He pulled her closer, wrapping himself around her as well. They were alone and adrift on a cabin cruiser with two dead, not knowing how long rescue would take, but warmth and a feeling of safety filled her when he wrapped her in his arms. The rain started, but they were dry under the cockpit cover. *Under other circumstances, this would be very nice.*

"So, why didn't they sink the boat? I mean, there's all this evidence."

"Usually, they want to send a message. Maybe this couple was taking drugs from the mother ship and delivering them to shore, for distribution. And, suppose they either didn't have the money or they shorted someone on the 'product.' The guys running the business want everybody else in the supply chain to know what happens if you try to cheat the boss."

"God. That's horrible."

"Yeah. But the people on the street who want drugs for their party – or habit, don't care about these people anyway. They just want their stuff."

Dawn broke and the sea was covered in fog. They stood and stretched. Scott started looking through cabinets. Just under the helm, he opened a cabinet and after a minute pulled out a small box.

"What's that?"

"Flare gun. If somebody gets close enough, we can alert them." He said it without emotion.

"You mean 'when,' not 'if' don't you?"

He looked at her, then, "Yes. Of course."

"Just making sure."

"If it's any comfort, while the Coast Guard might not care about a lowly enlisted man, they certainly wouldn't want to lose an officer."

He said it with a smile, but she felt a little stab as he pointed out the barrier between them, as if they were different species. She walked to the stern and stared out into the fog.

Two hours later, the fog was clearing with the sun's heat. An hour after that, the sound of a helicopter in the distance. Scott loaded the flare gun and shot a flare into the sky. They watched as the glowing red ball flew more than a hundred feet into the air, then arched and slowly dropped into the sea. Ten seconds later, he repeated the process. The sound of the aircraft became reassuringly louder. A Coast Guard HH 65 Dolphin helicopter appeared overhead.

They waved, then Scott put his hand to his ear, pantomiming using a radio. A minute later, a hand held radio was lowered in a bag. Scott took it, and the helicopter backed away so the sound of the engines and rotor would not be too strong for communication.

She listened to him talking to the aircraft, although she only got half of the conversation.

"Nice to see you."

"Yesterday at dusk."

"Surprised us with an RPG and automatic weapons."

"Yeah. Probably drug runners. Two bodies onboard. Male and female."

"We're okay for now. The lieutenant got a pretty good bump on her head, but she seems okay."

"Okay. We'll wait for the surface craft to take over the boat. Thanks."

The helicopter returned overhead. A second bag appeared and came down. It contained a thermos of coffee and sandwiches.

"God bless those guys."

The crew chief waved and the helicopter headed off in the direction of land, even though land was now out of sight. Two hours later, a Coast Guard cutter steamed up to the drifting boat. A party of four boarded. Scott asked that Dee be examined because of her head injury. While that was being done, he briefed them and showed them the bodies. After communication back and forth with the cutter, a line was tied to the bow of the civilian boat and the stern of the cutter. Scott and Dee transferred to the cutter and were welcomed aboard. They were given a cursory exam by the enlisted medic and put into separate cabins for the ride home.

Thirty

Annie opened the door to the hospital room where Dee was the only occupant. Dee was reclining on the bed with her eyes closed, but when she heard the door open, she looked over.

"Hi. Thanks for coming. It gets pretty lonely here. They won't even let me read or watch TV."

"Well, you look good. How long until you get paroled?"

"They said they want to keep me one more night. Observation. It was a bump on the head."

"Yeah, but I think it was a little more than a bump on the head."

"I'm kind of surprised that he hasn't been to see me. I hope he's okay."

"Yeah, about that –"

The door opened and a nurse came in. She took Dee's vital signs and did a quick visual acuity test. Then, she asked Dee her name, who the President was, and the date.

"The same as they were an hour ago," she answered in somewhat of a huff.

"Just doing my job, lieutenant. Maybe I should report an aggravated patient – sign of a brain injury – needs another couple of days to be sure she's okay. By the way,

I have the next two days off." She had a wan smile on her face.

Dee rattled off the information requested and the nurse left.

"I just want *out* of this place," she said to Annie.

"Got it. So, what happened?"

"I'm not sure I really know. We were headed along the coast. Scott wanted me to do some night navigation."

"More like submarine races if you ask me."

"Shush! It wasn't that way. Anyway, just before sunset, we spotted this cabin cruiser – and decided to take a look. All of a sudden, he yelled something. I heard a whoosh and a couple of shots, he moved the helm, and my world went dark until I woke up on the boat – the cabin cruiser, ours had apparently sunk – sometime in the night. He'd found a blanket he'd wrapped around us – and kept me warm with his body."

Annie cocked one eyebrow.

"Oh my God! If anything ever did happen between us, you'd be insufferable. It's not like he could build a fire on the boat to keep us warm."

"Uh huh. So, then what?"

She explained about the bodies and her vomiting, as well as their eventual rescue. "Once we got onto the cutter, they separated us and I haven't seen him since. I thought he might stop by – you know to see how the OIC is doing."

"Yeah. The OIC. Well, I was –"

There was a knock on the door. Dee told whoever it was to enter. It was a very young-looking Coast Guard lieutenant junior grade, or jg. He was in dress uniform, his combination cap under his left arm and an envelope in his right hand.

"Good afternoon, ma'am. My name is Harlan Spicer. You are Lieutenant Dee Cruise?"

"Yes," she said, anxiety growing within her.

"This is for you, ma'am," he said handing her the envelope. "There is to be an official inquiry – marine board of inquiry – into the sinking and loss of the Coast Guard response boat with the identification listed on the inquiry order. You shall make yourself available at the dates, times, and place for that inquiry. Any questions should be referred to the office of the Judge Advocate General."

Before Dee could respond, he turned on his heel and departed.

Slowly, she lifted the envelope and stared at it, her vision unfocused. When Annie moved in her chair, she jumped. She was dizzy and her stomach churned. *An inquiry? What if they find it was all my fault? What if – what if they bring charges? My god!*

"Dee! Dee!" It was Annie watching her friend sink into apparent despair.

She jumped, again. "What?!"

"Easy. Take it easy."

"I – I can't. What if they find it was all my fault? It's not just my career, but maybe his too."

"Whoa! Slow it down. It's an inquiry. You lost a boat – a relatively expensive boat. Not like the Titanic or anything, but still, when an expensive piece of equipment doesn't come back, there has to be some official explanation. This is how they do it with a sinking. You can't just come back, throw up your hands and go, 'Oopsie, we went out and the boat sank. Oh, well,' and have them accept that."

"I know. It's just – my dad. He never thought women should be doing anything but 'girly' things. Sometimes he'd set up what he considered man's work for me. It wasn't until much later that I realized each one of those was designed to make me fail. Show me my place. Even knowing it, I still panic at the thought of failing."

"It's not going to be that way."

"Yeah, but – Where's Scott?"

"Oh, yeah. Scott. Well, it seems that until the marine board of inquiry is completed, at least until the testimony is complete, he's been temporarily transferred."

She was in a daze. "W-h-a-t?"

"Yeah. Um, they talked to him this morning – at the station. They apparently want to get each of your versions without the two of you talking about what happened and coming up with a combined version. They want independent testimony. They do it all the time." It sounded lame and Annie wasn't looking at Dee.

"This is worse than I thought. Scott saved me. What if – what if I say something that will get him into trouble. I mean, I am worried about my career, but I don't want to say or do anything that will mess his up. I couldn't live with myself."

"Well, I've got one suggestion. First, stop referring to him as Scott. It's Chief Jackson. If you're giving your statement and call him Scott, it may open a line of investigation that could send both of you to jail."

Thirty-one

Dee walked into her office. It was the first day after her release from the hospital and she'd been cleared to return to full duty. She looked around. This was the same placed she'd been only a few days ago, but it was foreign and cold. The effect of the sinking, trauma, and hospital stay had changed things. Because of her, Scott – the chief – was now elsewhere and that made her feel like an outsider. She was alone and worried. A marine board of inquiry. It could be the end of her career. Scott – the chief – wasn't there and wasn't going to be there. He was somewhere else. *I wonder how he's doing. I wonder if he misses me.*

Annie came in, closed the office door and plopped into a chair. "So, how you doing?"

"How am I doing? I sank a boat, may lose my career, and made it so the chief they all worship is gone. I'm doing terrible. I can't stop thinking about this board. I'm terrified. All I've wanted was a career. And, now it may be gone."

"Wow. Talk about a negative Nancy."

Dee glared.

"Look. This may not be easy, but you should listen. Sacred or not, would the career officer you want to be just roll over and die? Hell no. And you're not going to. The board will take two weeks, tops. So, in that two weeks, you've got to be the strong lieutenant who can defend anything that happened to the board and run this place efficiently. That's not only what you should do, that's what Scott would want you to do, as well. He's not always going to be around to help you out. He wants you to be the officer and leader you want and need to be. Look at this as a learning experience."

Dee stared. "That's not going to be easy."

"Of course, it's not going to be easy. It's a test. The universe wants to know if you have what it takes to be the person you say you want to be. To have the things you want, you have to do the things you've never done and become the person you never were. I'm here to help, so let's get to it."

"Okay. You're here to help. Help me get the lay of the land."

"It's only going to be two weeks – tops," said Annie. "Scott isn't here, but they aren't sending a temporary chief while he's gone. Got that from headquarters admin. That in itself could be good news. It's like they expect that he'll return once the board finds no fault."

"Okay. I'll want the org chart. While he's gone, the department heads will report directly to me. Let's set a meeting for 10 AM. They'll need to update me on what's going on. It will have to be in depth because I don't have all the information that Scott – Chief Jackson already has. You join us too."

"Okay. One other thing. Morale is low, as you might expect. I've got a couple of things I absolutely need to get done. I lost some time visiting a malingering friend in the hospital." She smiled. "Could you run out to get a couple dozen donuts. I wouldn't ask, but it might help lift spirits."

Dee's spirit sank. The last thing she wanted to do was head out for donuts, but Annie might be right. Donuts might boost the spirits, if only a little.

"Oh, yeah. Tony's is closest, but the place two blocks further down is much better. With any luck, you might catch them with the red light on. Man! Those are good donuts. Please?"

"I'm beginning to wonder whose spirits are going to be lifted the most by this donut run," Dee said with a smile.

"That's my girl."

She pulled out of the parking lot and headed toward what they euphemistically called 'town.' There was a total of six traffic lights between the station and the donut shop that Annie had raved about. She managed to miss five of the six. "Well, this doesn't bode well."

When she looked at the façade, the red light was not on. Her shoulders dropped. She pulled the door open and entered the shop, walking to the counter. A middle-aged woman in a white shirtwaist uniform dress greeted her.

"Hi hon! What can I get you?"

"Uh, I guess I'd like two dozen. Just mix them up."

"Good. Oh, if you aren't in a huge hurry, we'll have a fresh batch coming out in a couple of minutes. They're always better when they're fresh."

"Sure. Why not?" She shrugged.

"Coffee? How about a cup on the house while you wait?"

"Okay."

The woman walked to the coffee machine and poured a cup. She set it on the counter. "Take anything in it?"

A voice from behind her said, "I believe the lady takes two cream and half a Splenda."

She spun around and saw him standing behind her. Faded jeans, sweatshirt, and boots. "How? Where?" Then she grabbed and hugged him. "Oh my god! I am SO happy to see you."

"He put his arms around her and said, "Me too. Let's take the coffee into the corner."

The walked to a booth in the corner. She slid in, and he slid in next to her. He had half a cup of coffee sitting on the table.

"This has got to be hard on you. How are you holding up?" he asked.

"I'm not sure. Annie gave me a pep talk this morning, then told me it would help spirits if I got donuts. I thought it was crap, but I have to admit, my spirits soared when I heard you behind me. She's devious."

"She's sweet. I didn't want you to think I didn't care. We need to be careful. They want to keep us separated – so we can't coordinate our stories. It's routine, but it adds extra stress. I want to be sure you're okay."

"I know, but I – I – I don't know. I don't want to say anything that would hurt you – you know, your career. To tell you the truth, I don't remember much." She smiled and said, "Somebody knocked me out. I'm not sure he wasn't getting me back for something I did earlier."

"Don't worry about me. Just tell the truth. First, it's easier to remember. Second, if the truth is going to hurt me, so be it. I don't believe it will. We didn't do anything wrong."

"I can't believe how empty and dead the station feels without you."

"It won't be long, and I miss you too, but you'll be fine. Ayala will take care of the rescue operations and maintenance. Jonesy will head up medical. You should get daily reports from them. Annie can help you with the admin stuff. This is kind of like throwing you into the deep end, but I know you're up to it. You're a good officer. Now, I should get going before we're busted."

He slid out of the booth and looked around. When he turned to say goodbye, she was standing next to him and put her arms around him. "I –"

"Yeah." He held her for a minute, then, "Looks like your donuts are ready. And remember, you're as good as the best thing you've ever done."

She kissed him softly on the lips. He looked at her for a full minute. She saw a softness and sadness in his eyes. And something else.

He smiled slightly, then turned and left.

She walked to the counter feeling light.

The woman put the two dozen donuts on the counter. "How was the coffee?"

"Great. I don't think I've ever enjoyed a cup of coffee as much as I did this one. How much?"

"The gentleman paid. Even gave me a great tip. By the way, he's a keeper."

"What? No. We're just – "

"Hon, I may not have a college degree, but I can tell when a man is in love. Didn't see it so much when he came in, but I sure did when he left. In his eyes. You may think you're just whatever, but he's in love."

Dee blushed, doubled the tip, left the store, loaded the warm donuts into the passenger side and drove back to the station – making every single light and humming all the way. She kept thinking about what the clerk said.

When she arrived, she put the donuts out and told the closest coast guardsman to spread the word.

Annie entered her office. "Okay, the meeting's set. How did the trip for the donuts go? You seem to be in better spirits since you returned."

"It was wonderful. I was so happy to see him. He made me feel like everything is going to be fine. I don't know how he does it, but it's like he infuses confidence and strength."

"Yeah. I'd like to have him infuse me. But then, I guess we're talking about two different infusions."

"It wasn't that way."

"Sure. Platonic all the way," Annie said deadpan.

"Well," Dee said, closing one eye and tilting her head.

The rest of the day was busy. She got a report from petty officers Ayala and Jones. They knew what they were doing. *I wonder if they give daily reports to Scott – the chief. I'm going to have to control that.* Before she knew it, the time was late, and almost everyone was gone.

Annie entered. "You should get out of here. First day of the board is tomorrow. They'll just do some preliminaries. You won't have to testify for a couple of days or so, but you'll still need your beauty sleep and be ready to sit in the room – it's in your best interest to hear everything."

"Yes. I know. To tell you the truth, I'm a little scared."

"That's only natural. If they were discussing my latest trip to the grocery store, I'd be nervous. Right now, I'd be pretty much worthless. But you're an officer – and a good one. Being effective when you're scared comes with the territory, but I'm sure you can handle it."

Buoyed by both Scott's and Annie's confidence, and happy that she'd been able to see Scott, if only for a few minutes, she went home in good spirits. She parked her vehicle and walked to her apartment. Closing and locking the door, the fears started to return. She showered and had one glass of wine. She sat thinking about the surprise this morning. Warmth spread within her. She smiled. Her career was still of utmost importance, but with everything going on, it was so great to see him. Finally, with her wine gone and the stress of the day and fatigue taking its toll, she went to bed.

Thirty-two

Dee parked her SUV and climbed the stairs of the Spanish Colonial headquarters building. She walked across the open patio and paused a moment to look at the Pacific, the water blue in the bright late August sunlight. She walked under the portico and into the building. It took a few minutes to find the conference room that would serve as the appointed place for the Marine Board of Inquiry. Outside the room was a sign announcing the board and stating 'Authorized Personnel Only.' When she'd arrived here a few months ago, in early June, there was a feeling of excitement and anticipation in her. The start of her new adventure. Now, as August was in its last days, there was worry and loneliness.

She sat alone in the last row of seats. In front of the small seating area a table with a single chair faced the front of the room. Across from and facing it, on a dais, was a table with three chairs – for the board members. To the left side of the room was a table with a single chair. Here is where the legal officer would sit to ensure the proceedings were done in keeping with judicial standards. On the other side of the room, against the wall, was a small table and chair. A few lights were on, but the room felt cold, dark, and lonely. Annie and Scott both said this was routine. Why don't I feel routine? Maybe I'm not really the right stuff. Maybe they're wrong and I'm not cut out to be an officer.

She jumped when the lights came on. An enlisted petty officer third class wheeled in a small cart. Water pitchers and classes were placed at the three places on table in front, the table to the left and the one to the right. A single pitcher was placed on the witness table. Six glasses were placed there. Upside down. Writing tablets and pens were placed on the board table. The petty officer left without acknowledging her.

Ten minutes later, people started filing in, taking seats. Some were in uniform, some in civilian attire – suits for both the men and women. She was glad she'd worn her dress uniform rather than the summer uniform that was prescribed for this time of year. The door behind the table where the panel would sit opened and a commander entered. He held a large case in his hand and moved to the table reserved for the legal counsel. A young woman in civilian attire entered the door she had used and walked to the table directly across from the legal officer's place. She removed something from a case she was carrying and set it on the table. Dee recognized it as a court reporter's stenotype keyboard. Two lieutenant commanders entered through the back door. Their uniforms were impeccable. They were talking quietly between themselves. They moved to the board table.

Well, there are two of the three. I wonder who –

Just then, the back door opened again, and Captain Trahir entered. The two lieutenant commanders came to immediate attention. Captain Trahir looked around the room, pretending not to see the two junior men standing rigidly.

Same crap he pulled with me.

He walked to the legal officer who looked up from unloading the items from his bag, and when he had the legal officer's attention, shook his hand. The legal officer exchanged a few words with him and returned to his work.

Trahir walked to the table and engaged the two more junior officers, pretending he hadn't seen them at rigid attention. He chatted with them, but it was clear to her that these two knew Trahir controlled their careers and future.

Well, I guess I know who will be making all the decisions.

Trahir looked at the clock on the wall, walked to the table, picked up a gavel and tapped it until he had silence. "If we can all take our seats."

Everyone moved to a seat. She was glad to be hidden in back, although she knew she would be sitting at that table in a day or two.

Trahir looked at the silent audience for more than a minute.

God, he's relishing being the man in charge. He's actually performing! What an —

"Ladies and gentlemen, my name is Captain Franklin Trahir, and I am the convening authority for this Marine Board of Inquiry in the case of the response boat number 26215 which was lost as sea on August 16th of this year — in order to make a determination regarding the manner of that loss. Lieutenant Commanders Smith and Hayes will assist in making that determination. While this is not a trial, Commander Philips of the Office of the Judge Advocate General is here to ensure that the proceedings are completed in a fair and legal manner because the outcome may have significant impact on the careers of Coast Guard personnel. I now declare this Marine Board of Inquiry open."

Dee slumped in her seat. She dropped her head. She was dizzy. Her throat was tightening. She wanted to cry, but she was afraid everyone would see her.

The first witness to give testimony was the captain of the vessel that rescued her and Scott the morning after. "We found the boat, a 45-foot Tiara Sovran, adrift ten miles off shore." He gave the coordinates. "Two Coast Guard personnel were onboard at the time along with a male and female – deceased. The Coast Guard personnel were Chief Petty Officer Scott Jackson and Lieutenant Dee Cruise, both attached to Sandy Point Station. Our corpsman made a cursory examination of those individuals and we transported them to shore. In the cockpit of the cabin cruiser were 217 empty casings, caliber," he consulted a small notebook, "7.62 by 39, consistent with a Kalashnikov assault rifle. Chief Jackson stated he heard a whoosh just before the rifle fire started. We did not find a launch tube for a rocket propelled grenade, although it may have been dropped over board or –"

"Thank you, captain," Trahir interrupted. "If you didn't find it, you didn't find it. No need to testify about something when there is no evidence that it actually existed."

What! Is he doubting what we both put into our written statements? What's going on?

"Yes, sir. The only thing I have to add is that a male body was found inside the cabin and a female on the bow, covered with a blanket. They were left in place until we returned to port. The FBI and DEA were called and took possession of the bodies and boat."

"Thank you, captain. You are excused. Our next witness is Dr. Kathryn Christopher."

The captain of the rescue ship got up and walked to the back of the room, picking up a briefcase before leaving. A slight, middle-aged woman took his place.

"Dr. Christopher, thank you for coming today. Would you please tell us what you found?"

"Yes, for the record, my name is Kathryn Christopher, I am a physician, board certified pathologist and the medical examiner for the Federal Bureau of Investigation in this geographic area. Two bodies were delivered to me on August 17th of this year. One was a male, age determined to be 36 years after he was identified by his fingerprints. The other, female, 32 years. She was identified by a driver's license. The female had been sexually assaulted multiple times, before –"

Dee left her seat, willing herself not to listen to the testimony of the medical examiner. She had been on the boat with these people – even if they had been dead when she was there. It was too raw. She needed air. She didn't want to know the grisly details, even if they were delivered — well maybe *because* they were delivered in a cold, clinical manner. She'd seen the man. He haunted her in nightmares. She couldn't imagine what he had suffered before he'd finally been killed. She didn't want to know. What in the hell had they been thinking? It had brought them to a terrible end. Dee knew the woman must have been raped. Multiple times. The medical examiner could probably tell how many times and by how many men. Had they given her hope? 'You do this and we'll let you live.' Or had they just held her down? Was he alive to watch? Probably. More cruel that way. She shook her head. *Stop! Stop! Stop!*

People were coming out of the room. She looked at her phone. She realized she'd lost an hour, standing on the balcony and staring at the ocean. Thinking about — things. It was time for lunch. She wasn't hungry. She overheard two of the women talking as they left.

"Well, I guess we don't have to be back until tomorrow. I can use the time to get some things done in the office."

She returned to the now almost empty room. The board members were gone, but the attorney was still there, packing up his case.

"Excuse, me, commander, I was in the ladies' room when the meeting adjourned. Is it over for the day?"

"Yes, it is," he was looking over his glasses at her uniform, she guessed to determine her rank and probably her name. "The board will reconvene at 10 AM tomorrow, Lieutenant, uh, Cruise. Apparently, the chair had some pressing business to take care of this afternoon."

"Uh, thank you." She made her way to her vehicle and headed back to the station. She was in a daze. Vehicle horns were honking. She jumped, then realized she'd run a red light without seeing it. She had to get control of herself.

Thirty-three

Dee sat in the small audience area. It was ten minutes to ten in the morning – the second day of the inquiry. People were filing in slowly. The legal officer entered, went to his table, and started unpacking his bag – legal pads, pens, laptop, and a couple of weighty books. The recorder also entered and took her place and set up her stenotype machine. The two lieutenant commanders who were on the inquiry board entered.

At two minutes of ten Captain Trahir entered. He was carrying a briefcase, which he set on the table. The two lieutenant commanders came to attention immediately when they saw him. As before, he ignored them for a few minutes, then, as if he was surprised they were at attention, he told them to relax. They relaxed only a bit and it seemed evident to Dee they were still essentially at attention, probably afraid to relax completely around him.

Trahir shuffled papers for a bit, then pulled out a folder and set his briefcase on the floor.

"This Marine Board of Inquiry is now in session. Our first witness is Mr. Robert White. Mr. White. Please."

An African American man in a tailored blue suit got up from his seat in the back of the room and walked to the witness table. He pulled the chair back and sat. His posture was erect, almost military in bearing. Without unbuttoning his coat, he reached into an interior pocket and removed a folded document.

"My name is Robert White. I am an administrator for the Drug Enforcement Agency." He opened the document. "The two individuals on the cabin cruiser in this inquiry were a Mister John Michaels and a Miss Dawn Johnson. The two were cohabitating in the Los Angeles area, the precise location has not been disclosed due to the ongoing nature of the investigation."

Dee was fidgeting her hands nervously. A bird was flying around in her stomach. *Come on. I just want to get this over with. I wish I didn't have to testify at all.*

"The pair came to the attention of the DEA through an investigation by the Internal Revenue Service," White continued, "The two were apparently living beyond their means and had little reported income. Our investigation has found the two were involved in transporting illegal drugs from so-called mother ships to shore and then to individuals involved in the sale of the drugs to the public. Because of the ongoing nature of the investigation, that is all the agency is willing to disclose at this time."

He then folded the document and replaced it in his coat.

"Uh, thank you Agent," started Trahir.

"Mister," interrupted White.

Trahir stopped, seemingly surprised by the interruption. "Yes, Mister White."

White stood, straightened his coat, then walked to the back of the room and out the door.

Trahir seemed lost for a minute, staring at the door where the DEA man had left, then picked up papers from the desk and staring at those for longer than it seemed necessary.

"Our next witness is – Lieutenant Dee Cruise. Lieutenant Cruise to the table."

Is it just me, or did that seem cold? She stood. As she made her way to the aisle, she felt someone touch her shoulder. When she turned her head, she saw it was an enlisted man. He was holding a small envelope. She took the envelope and walked to the table. The bird in her stomach had turned into a flock. She approached the table and pulled back the chair. In the quiet room, the chair screeched across the floor, making her more conscious of people watching her. She sat and tried to look as military as she could.

Trahir was standing on the dais, his back to her. He studied a document he had picked up from the table, turned and looked at her, then looked at the document again.

If he's trying to get me even more nervous than I am, he's doing a great job.

She opened the envelope and pulled out a small note card. It read: 'You're a good officer. Don't let his theatrics unnerve you. Tell the truth – it will be your shield.' The handwriting was his. She put the card back into the envelope and held it in her fingers, drawing strength from it.

Trahir walked around behind the table, but remained standing. He was towering over her, his face a mask of judgement. "State your name and rank for the record."

"My name is Dee M. Cruise. I am a lieutenant in the United States Coast Guard."

"Lieutenant," he paused. "You were on the response boat number," he checked his papers, "26215 on August 16th of this year?"

"Yes, sir. Chief Jackson —"

"We'll get to that in due time, lieutenant. Just answer the question asked, unless you are specifically told to expound or give your version of events."

What is he trying to do? Frighten me? Make me say something that incriminates me? Or is this just more of him showing who is in charge? Well, he's not going to beat me up. I'm not going to play suck-up like his two lackeys.

"That morning, around 10 AM local time, you left to check on vessels – check on licenses, safety equipment, and the like?"

"Yes, sir."

"How many vessels did you check on?"

"I believe there were eight, sir. Not including the last, the one that attacked us."

Trahir gave her a withering look, as if she had disobeyed.

She ran her fingers over the envelope and sat even straighter in the chair. *He's not going to beat me down.*

"You found no violations?"

"No, sir."

"Personally?"

"I watched the chief, who did all the inspections on the other craft himself. I was at the helm of the response craft."

He looked at her again like she had approached or crossed some undefined line. Finally, "Why only two onboard. Don't missions generally have three personnel on the boat?"

"We were checking compliance with regulations – fishermen. A third person was not needed. In addition, we had an upcoming quarterly inspection of the station. We decided – I decided, *I will take credit for the decisions,* as officer in charge, that the water mission could be completed without a third person onboard."

"Ah, but that's the crux of it, isn't it? The mission wasn't completed successfully. That's why we are having this inquiry, isn't it lieutenant?"

"With all due respect, sir," *I probably shouldn't have said that. It'll just make him mad and he knows what I'm saying is not with all due respect.* "a third person on the boat would not have made any difference. Even if that third person were armed and had a weapon pointed at the boat, there wouldn't have been any time to respond because of the way we were attacked. A third person on the boat would only have put a third person at risk."

Trahir's face was red. His eyes narrowed. "This inquiry will decide whether you acted appropriately." His voice was cold and hard.

The rest of the morning's questions related to the compliance checks and why they had decided to wait to return after dark. All the questions were asked pointedly.

She was having to defend all of her decisions and actions. By the time the lunch break came, she was worn out. She left the witness table thinking she would have to change her uniform. The blouse she was wearing was damp. She'd sweat through it.

Annie met her on the portico. "You're doing great! He's being such an ass, but you're holding your own."

"Well, I don't feel like I'm holding my own. I'm surprised he hasn't made me justify why I chose the underwear I had on. By the way, where did the note come from? Well, I know where it came from. How did it get to me? By the way, it saved me more than once. Just having it in my fingers. Gave me strength."

"Yeah. We figured it might help. Seems like Trahir is out for blood. But why?"

Just then, Captain Trahir appeared with the two lieutenant commanders. Trahir was telling them some story, and the other two officers were laughing more than politely.

"The suck up brigade," said Annie. "Those two are out for promotion. Trahir can help them a little. He can hurt them a lot. I didn't mean – I'm sorry."

"No, you're right. He can hurt me a lot, too. I have an idea this is where this whole thing is going."

"No, there's something else. He's got another angle. Anyway, let's get you something to eat. Then, we need to do the locker room half-time pep talk."

"I'm not sure I won't throw up whatever we get to eat. And, I don't have any pep left."

"Well, I brought along an extra uniform, you know, just in case. And, I've got a salad – chicken Caesar or shrimp, whichever you prefer. And, some coffee – strong enough to raise the dead or kill the living."

"Annie, you're unbelievable. What would I do without you?"

Thirty-four

Dee spent the afternoon in the witness seat. Trahir seemed merciless in his questioning.

"Tell us again why you decided to run up the coast instead of returning home after the stated objective of the mission had been successfully completed. Why did you choose to open the port side window? Why did you remove your helmet during the mission? How far were you from the cabin cruiser when the attack started? Why did you delay evasive maneuvers? Why did you turn instead of confronting the attackers?"

On two occasions, the legal officer interrupted the questioning to state that the questions asked were outside the scope of the inquiry. Minor triumphs, she thought.

Finally, even Trahir seemed to have had enough. "I think that is all for today. If we need any further information, we will let you know when to return."

She was completely worn out. *I may actually have felt better after the attack and sinking than I do now.* She went to the restroom and splashed water on her face. *I can't wait to get home. I don't even have the energy for a hot bath. Home and bed.*

She pulled her SUV into her parking space and turned off the headlights and ignition. She patted the dash. "Just forty-eight more easy payments and you're all mine – I wonder what I'll be doing for a living then." It was getting dark. *Friday night. Date night. And I'm getting home for a nice lonely evening in front of the TV. Well, tomorrow I can sleep in.*

She dug in her purse for her keys. The small pepper spray canister was next to them. *I won't need it here. I'm home.* But she'd promised Scott. She pulled out the pepper spray and held it with her keys. She opened the door and slid out. A rumble of thunder in the distance caught her ear. *Better get inside.*

She was walking toward the entrance of her building when he spoke. "Well, good evening, Lieutenant. Working late?" She knew the voice without turning. *Captain Trahir.*

"Sir? What are you doing here?"

"I was in the area and wanted to check on you. I check on all my junior officers – periodically. You've had a tough day."

"Well, everything is fine. I should get inside. Looks like rain."

"Yes, if does, doesn't it?" He stepped closer, too close. "Perhaps I should come in and wait it out."

Dee's chest tightened. She began to feel cold and her insides were quivering. She looked quickly toward her door. "Uh, I don't think that would be such a good idea, sir. Especially with the inquiry and all. It wouldn't look right, sir." Thunder rumbled and she jumped.

"We're just two colleagues. You could offer me a drink. We can talk. You know, your testimony didn't really help your case today. It would seem you made a number of decisions that were – let's say, borderline. My decision on your actions could go either way at this time. It's important hat you remember just who has your career in their hands."

"This really isn't a good time, sir." *So, that is his game. Beat me up on the witness stand and have leverage against me. Play ball or lose my career.*

He stepped very close – too close. The smell of alcohol. "You don't need to use 'sir' when we're alone and off duty."

Thunder rumbled in the distance.

"Please, sir. You're making me feel uncomfortable."

"No need for that. You and I are going to be just fine. We're going to get to know each other – very well. The better I know you, the easier it will be to put this whole inquiry thing behind us."

"Is that what this is about? The 'friendlier' I am the easier the inquiry will go?" Anger suddenly burned deep within her.

A sudden rush of air blew through them.

"Well, that's not the way I would put it, but yes, lieutenant. Your being friendly will certainly speed the inquiry along to a conclusion that will be, how shall I say it, no impediment to your career." He stepped forward and grabbed her, trying to press his mouth against hers.

Dee shoved him. Her free hand slapped him – hard.

"Why you little," he hissed as he stepped in, towering over her.

Dee stepped back. The pepper spray discharged.

Trahir looked at it in her hand. His face twisted into a menacing mask. "So, that's the way you want it? You have no idea what you've just done. I've dealt with a hundred like you. The smart ones go along to get along. Their careers have flourished. The others? Let's just say they found the going impossible. They're all gone now. Make your plans for what you're going to do after this tour. I foresee a bad outcome for the inquiry and very poor marks on your fitness reports." He spit, turned, and disappeared into the dark.

Thunder crashed and she jumped.

Dee's hands trembled. She headed back to her car, leaning on it for support. Her legs were weak. The wetness of tears filled her eyes and her mouth was dry. She dropped her keys. She hung her head. *Oh my god! What have I –? I need to – Where did he go? Is he waiting out there? I need to get away.* A crash of thunder. She jumped. Dee looked in the direction of her apartment. *Is he there?* She grabbed her keys and hurried into her car. She grabbed her phone. Three tries later, she finally got the number right. As it rang, she looked at the skies hoping the storm would hold off for just a bit longer.

Thirty-five

She double checked the address she'd written on the scrap of paper. She thought she'd gotten it right. Her hand was shaking when she wrote it down. She took a deep breath, put the paper in her pocket, and knocked on the door.

The door opened. Scott's face appeared. His head tilted a bit to the right and he smiled slightly.

"Uh, hi. I —"

"Could I come in, please?" she asked.

"Of course. I'm sorry." His smile disappeared as he opened the door, then looked out as if to see if someone else was there. He stepped back inside, a look of concern on his face.

She entered and he closed the door. Lightning lit up the apartment. Two seconds later, a crack of thunder made her jump.

"You okay?"

"Yes. No. I don't know." She was trembling.

"Why don't I get you something to drink and you can tell me what has you – upset."

"Trahir."

"Captain Trahir?"

"Yes." She turned toward him. "He was at my apartment building. Tonight. He tried to – to –"

"He assaulted you."

"He got really close. I told him I was uncomfortable. Then, he grabbed me and tried to kiss me. I slapped him. He got really ugly and said my career is over. He's going to ruin me." Tears filled her eyes. "What am I going to do?"

"Okay. We can sort this out. Let me get you a drink. What would you like?"

A bolt of lightning lit up the sky. Two seconds later, the boom was so great glassware rattled, and her body shook. She jumped. Her head spun toward the window.

Scott took two steps toward her. "It's okay. You're okay. You're safe here."

Another flash. Another boom. Then, complete darkness as the power went out and the sound of heavy rain pounding on the roof began. She froze, then found him and curled into him.

He wrapped her in his arms, "It's okay. You're safe. Breathe."

His arms were around her. She was safe. *He'll protect me.* Her head was turned and pressed against his chest. She could feel his heart beating and the warmth of him against her. She uncoiled enough to put her hand on his chest. *Warmth. Strength.* The tension in her body eased a bit.

"Do you want to sit?"

"No. Just here. For a bit. Can I?"

"Yes."

After a few minutes, she relaxed slightly and he moved her to the couch. He sat her down and started to move away. She grabbed his arm.

"Stay. Please." Her request was quiet, plaintive.

He sat next to her and put his arm around her. She curled into him, pulling her legs up onto the couch and her arms into her stomach and chest. With each bolt of lightning and clap of thunder, she jumped. Slowly, the storm was starting to move on, the thunder and lightning more distant. Her breathing slowed and she closed her eyes. After a few minutes, she gave a couple of involuntary movements, and he knew that sleep was overtaking her.

It was an hour later when she moved that he slid his arms under her and started to pick her up. "I'm going to put you into bed. You'll be safe there. I'll be out here." He carried her into his bedroom, set her on the bed and removed her shoes before he pulled a blanket over her. He ran his hand softly over the side of her face, then turned and left the bedroom, closing the door behind him.

He walked to his hall closet and removed a pillow and blanket, then placed them on the couch. He dropped onto the couch and covered himself. The sounds of the storm now barely audible as he lay in the darkness and wondered what had happened to the world.

Thirty-six

She opened her eyes and looked around the room. *Where am I?* Then, she remembered, Trahir, the storm, coming here – to Scott's. She'd sat with him until – when? *I guess I fell asleep. This must be –*

She rolled her head around, taking in the room in its entirety. A window to her left. *Huh. Sheers. I wouldn't think a man would –* She turned to her right side. There was a picture on the wall and the entrance to what she guessed was the bath. She thought the picture – painting – was a copy of some impressionist's work. Renoir. A pond. *Something about frogs.* Under the picture was an antique Crosley floor console radio. At the end of the bed, a light-colored wood dresser with a black slate top. The bedside nightstands were of the same style. The bedside table lamps looked to be copies of work by Frank Lloyd Wright. *Impressive. Especially for a bachelor.*

She pulled the blanket off and sat on the edge of the bed. The floor was hardwood and a Persian rug – well, a look alike she was sure – covered most of the wood. *I wonder if he had a decorator. Don't be ridiculous. I'm sure a chief petty officer would have better things to do with whatever he makes than to hire a decorator. Annie must be wrong. I'll bet a woman did this. One he's kept secret. Maybe no longer around.* She felt a sinking within her and wondered why it should matter whether another woman was still around.

She opened the door and saw him standing by the breakfast bar, looking at a tablet. She was still tired and yawned.

"Well, good morning, sleepyhead." He was wearing a white t-shirt and faded jeans.

"Good morning to you, too."

"Interested in something to eat?"

"Depends if you're a decent cook." She laughed, then, "Please. How long have I been out?"

"About nine hours."

"Well, I guess I was –" she spotted the pillow and folded blanket on the couch. "You didn't sleep on the couch, did you?"

"It's not bad. And, it's better than the floor."

"I can't believe you slept on the couch."

"Not many choices, you know."

She turned bright red as she thought of the only other real choice. "Well, I could have slept out here – there," she said pointing to the couch.

"It made the most sense. Anyway, breakfast, eggs?"

"Well, I shouldn't say it, but I'm famished." She looked toward the bedroom. "Would it be okay if I took a shower?"

"Sure. There's a robe. We can run your things through the wash. Cycle's pretty quick. They should be done and dry by the time you're done eating."

"Um, sure. Okay." She returned in a minute wearing a robe, her clothes in her hand. "Where do you want these?"

"Here." He opened a small door by the pantry. An over-under washer dryer were stacked inside.

She placed her clothes into the washer, and he added the detergent. He closed the lid, started the washer, then closed the door.

Thirty-seven

As she'd headed back to the bedroom, he'd watched the way her anatomy moved inside the robe. All he could think was 'poetry in motion.' He shook his head and started to pull out the things he would need to make the meal. *Trahir. What kind of commanding officer –* He shook his head. They'd have to report it. *Question is, will they believe it?*

As he stood in the kitchen prepping for breakfast, he sipped his coffee. There was a knock on the door. When he opened it, Angela Jones was standing outside.

"Good morning. Come on in. Coffee?"

"No, thanks. I just stopped by to see if you still wanted to go through the supplies today. Last night's storm pretty well wet everything down."

"Yeah, here too. Lost power until about 5 this morning. Anyway, something came up last night that I'm going to need to take care of today. How about tomorrow? Eight or nine?"

"You know chief, you're just lucky I don't have a life. Why don't we make it nine? Give me a chance to sleep in – as if!" She left and closed the door behind her.

Dee came out of the bedroom wearing a white terrycloth robe and had a towel wrapped around her head.

He smiled. "Good morning again."

She smiled in return. "Good morning again to you."

"Coffee?"

"Please."

He poured a cup, added two French vanilla creamers and half a package of Splenda, and handed it to her.

The door opened and Angela poked her head in. "Oh, by the way, the L T called last night. Wanted your address. I figured – OH HELL NO!"

"Uh, Jonesy, it's not what you think."

"What I think is you've got a freshly showered female officer standing in your living room wearing nothing but a robe and a towel."

"Okay. Maybe it is what you think. I can explain."

"I'm not sure I want to know. It may make me an accomplice – after the fact. I know that I definitely don't want to know what might have happened before the shower."

"Captain Trahir assaulted me last night," said Dee quietly, stopping Angela in her tracks. "At my building. I didn't feel safe there. The only thing I could think of was to come here."

Angela entered and shut the door behind her.

"Have a seat Jonesy. Coffee?"

"Coffee, hell. I'm going to need something a lot stronger than coffee for this. Maybe I can tell the judge I was hallucinating. Uh, no Your Honor, I had been drinking and I'm not exactly sure what I saw. Gimmee some of that good scotch of yours. Three fingers – your fingers, not hers. No offense ma'am."He went to a cabinet, opened it and pulled out a bottle. He poured two fingers of scotch into a Glencairn glass and handed it to her. She looked at the amount.

"Two fingers is the most you can get into that glass. Reasonably."

"If you've got a paper cup, I could get more in," she said with a smile.

"If you did that, I'd have to shoot you."

Angela looked at Dee, "Okay, now I really don't want to know what happened before the shower. When the chief hands over a glass of $2000 scotch without an argument, I know something happened before the shower." She turned to the chief, "If it did, I'll say you've got great taste in officers, just before they hang you. If nothing happened, you still have great taste, but you're an idiot – all due respect." She sipped the scotch. "Man! That's good."

"Was that a complement?" asked Dee.

"Uh, yeah," he said. "But we've still got to figure out what we're going to do."

"He said he was going to ruin my career. He said I had to go along to get along. And, that nobody would believe me – when he denied it all."

"We need to have you call the NCIS agent. The one you gave your statement to after you were drugged at the club. That's the only thing that makes sense."

"So, you gonna go with the system?" It was Angela.

"I don't see any other choice. Much as I'd like to, we can't just run him down. With any luck, there might have been other women he's tried this with who have complained."

"Fine. I guess as long as my career is over anyway, I might as well do this. Let me get dressed."

"You know, chief, there's something that I'm just dying to say, but I think I'll just finish my drink and leave."

"Good choice Jonesy."

Ten minutes later, Dee was talking with the NCIS agent who took her statement over the phone. She had to go through it three times. Each time, the agent asked more questions. The agent thanked her for the information. There was no need for a trip to the hospital since there was no actual physical evidence. When she'd finished, she cut the connection and sat dejectedly. An emptiness filled her. "Everything I've worked for –"

"We don't know that for sure."

"He was right. Nobody will believe me. They'll pass it off as another woman trying to cause trouble for a – a respected senior officer."

"I'm going to take a quick shower. I hope you ladies will be okay for a few minutes." He left the room.

"We need to talk," said Angela. "I don't know what happened last night."

"Well, I –"

"You misunderstand. I don't want to know what happened last night. But, here's the deal. The chief got me to apply for college. I was really nervous, so he held my hand for the interview – not literally. He filled out all the forms so I could get financial aid – basically a free education. I get nothing but A's. Not 'cuz I'm smart, but because I don't want to let him down. When some of the troops can't meet their rent or don't have food, money magically appears. Any one of us would die for that man, so if you screw him up – and I'm not just talking about his career – which could go down the crapper from this – the whole thing with Captain Trahir will be a minor problem compared with what you'll be dealing with. Am I clear – ma'am?"

"Perfectly. And I have no intention of causing him any harm – in any way."

Thirty-eight

"Okay. So, Captain Trahir accosted you at your place," said Annie.

"Yes." She turned away.

"And you slapped him, then shot him with pepper spray."

"Well, he grabbed me." She turned back, her face set. "I was scared. Yes, I slapped him. The pepper spray was in my hand with my keys. It went off. I don't know if it even hit him. It's not like I shot him or anything."

"But see, the problem is that he's still in charge of the inquiry board. Well, I assume he is. He can make it go either way."

"So, what your saying is that I should have let him," said Dee.

"No. Maybe there was a better way to say no."

"I tried to tell him no. He said being friendly would make the inquiry go better for me. He grabbed me! Maybe I could have vomited on him. God knows I felt like it." Dee's body deflated.

"Well, that might have worked," said Annie.

"Yeah, great. I wonder if they need anybody down at the donut shop. I have an idea I'm going to need a job after this is over."

"It just seems so strange. I mean Trahir is really going over a line. He has a career to lose, too, you know."

"It's like he said. Who's going to believe a lieutenant being investigated for the possible loss of a boat because of – basically dereliction of duty. He can claim that I came on to him. That I propositioned him to make the whole thing go away. Even if he doesn't report it now, he can claim later that he didn't want an investigation of my behavior to influence his judgement in the inquiry. No. I'm screwed." Dee was looking at the floor and shook her head slowly.

"Scott – you remember – the chief? Well, he still has to testify. I think he'll do okay. He'll show Trahir that everything was done for a reason."

"Trahir still makes the decisions – and writes the report." She dropped into a chair. "He can write it anyway he wants. He can make it look like every decision I made was wrong. Not just wrong, bad. And, I'm sure my fitness report will be bottom of the heap. Unless there is some kind of miracle, my career is over."

"Well, let's listen to what Scott has to say."

"How?"

"Same way I listened to you. There's a little side room with a speaker. We can sit there and listen in."

"Well, it doesn't make me feel any better, but I do want to listen to him – maybe just hearing his voice will make it better. I wonder how Trahir will treat him."

Thirty-nine

Scott Jackson sat at the witness table. Annie and Dee were in a small side room listening in to his testimony. After giving his name and rank, he slowly poured himself a glass of water during Captain Trahir's first question.

"Chief Jackson, what was the purpose of the excursion on August 16th?"

"It was a routine mission. We periodically go out to make – you might call them welfare checks – on boats on the water."

"Welfare checks?"

"Yes sir. We make sure they have their licenses, registrations, safety equipment. That kind of thing."

"How many people are usually assigned?"

"We usually do the checks with two individuals. One to run the boat and one to do the inspections."

"Do you usually take an officer, the OIC, with you when you do these checks?"

"No, sir. To be honest, the OICs I've served with in the past have not been interested. LT Cruise wanted to know first-hand what we did on the checks. She decided to observe and participate."

"And did this hamper you?"

"No, she did not," answered Scott. "In fact, I have a great deal of respect for an officer who wants to see what is done and how and not just have faith that all assigned tasks are being done as they should. The lieutenant is not afraid of getting her hands dirty to learn the nuts and bolts."

In the small side room, Dee leaned over to Annie, "What's he trying to do?"

"Trahir is trying to get him to say anything that would make it seem like you shouldn't have been there. Or your decisions weren't good."

"Thank you, chief, but I will ask that you keep personal opinion to yourself." Now, why didn't you have a third person on the boat? A third person might have engaged to adversaries and you wouldn't have lost a boat."

"I do not believe a third person would have helped, sir. First, we approached a cabin cruiser that had fishing poles off the stern, appeared to have a woman sunbathing on the bow, and a man waving to us from the cockpit. We don't approach a vessel on a welfare check with guns drawn and at the ready. A third person on our craft wouldn't have been aiming a loaded weapon at them, and that is the only way we could have even remotely had a chance to answer the attack. In view of the speed and vicious nature of the attack, I don't believe even an armed and ready coastguardsman would have staved it off."

"Shouldn't you have done a 360, that is, circled the craft before approaching?"

"We generally do 360s closer than we were, maybe twenty-five yards out, and we do them for apparently abandoned craft, not those with sunbathers and waving passengers."

"And yet," Trahir said smugly, "it was a trap you fell for."

"Yes sir, it was a trap. One that almost caught us. Luckily, they got jumpy and shot their RPG early. And missed."

"No launcher was found for an RPG. An RPG is a supposition on your part."

"No sir. I spent a number of years in drug interdiction. I've been shot at a number of times and had at least six RPGs shot at me. If you'd ever heard one go off close to you – or at you, you wouldn't have any doubt." He held Trahir's eyes, challenging him. *Trahir - an administrative officer. His record shows he's had almost no operational experience. Then, too, he seems brave enough when he's forcing himself on junior female officers.* "Most of these guys are bad shots, especially on the water. I saw a tube and heard the missile. They may have taken the tube with them."

Trahir seemed taken aback. Then, "Very well. You decided to swim to the boat."

"Yes, sir, it was the only way we would stay alive through the night." He described swimming to the boat and getting Dee aboard. His descriptions were accurate except that he downplayed any heroism on his part and kept insisting that he and LT Cruise worked as a team to secure the scene and survive the night. There was no mention of her getting sick and vomiting after seeing the corpse of the male, and he again stressed that she played a major part in their rescue the next morning. When asked about the lieutenant's decisions and judgement, he stated that they were appropriate and consistent with current practice and Coast Guard regulations.

After three hours, Trahir, the Inquisitor, seemed to be more worn out than the witness. "Thank you, Chief Jackson. I believe we have all the information we need – for now. If we need additional testimony, we will let you know."

"I'll be happy to add any clarification that you might want, captain," he said.

Next door, Annie and Dee sat quietly for a moment.

"He made it seem like I did at least half the work," Dee said. "I was useless. I didn't make any of the good decisions he talked about."

"I told you when you got here, the chief could help you or hurt you. Apparently, he has decided you are worth helping. Besides, I don't know what he's thinking, but you were there with him. He probably wants to make sure you get credit for being there and doing what you could. He doesn't want to give Trahir any indication that you weren't the effective officer in charge."

"I don't know if that is right. And, I don't know if it will actually do any good. Trahir may just decide to sink my career."

Forty

Scott sat in his truck. He loosened his tie and opened the collar of his shirt. He was tired. The day had worn him out, but he hadn't caved. His hatred for Trahir and what Trahir tried to do to Dee kept him going. Said some things that had surprised Trahir, and at least a couple of things that made him real mad. Brought up the fact that he doesn't have any real operational experience, yet here he is passing judgement on an operation. *Shouldn't have said what I did, but thinking about him and what he'd intended for her, I lost it. At least for the moment. Got to be careful about not doing that again. If there even is an again.*

She'd passed every test he'd given her. Some of those weren't really so fair, either. She did okay on those, and she proved that she was a good officer – out to do her best for the service. *Unlike Trahir, she's a shipmate and deserves to be treated like one. That means we live or die for each other. And, right now, Trahir's the enemy. I wonder what the son of a bitch has up his sleeve.*

He needed a shower – needed to get cleaned up. Cooking was out. He'd order in – if he could stay awake that long. He thought about the day and the board. *Maybe it's time I left this outfit. There are a few things you should be able to count on – like your commanding officer not raping you.* There has to be a way to get that bastard. *I'm not sure I can change anything. And, I'm not sure at all that I'm doing her any good. I'm not helping her career. She deserves a shot.*

He started the truck and drove slowly out of the parking lot, oblivious to his speed. The ride home took longer than usual, although he wasn't really paying attention. He was lost in thought. He parked the truck, turned off the engine and closed the garage door with the remote. *Maybe nothing to eat tonight. Shower. Maybe a drink. And bed.*

Forty-one

Scott opened the door, stepped into his dark apartment, closed the door, and leaned back against it.

"Don't turn on the light. For the moment, I want it dark," said Dee.

He said nothing.

"You know, leaving a key under your mat isn't really a very safe place. Anybody could have found it, come in, robbed the place, or killed you in your sleep."

"When I was a boy," he said, "– between middle school and high school – summer break, there was a girl. To me, she was the most beautiful girl in the world. I was smitten. Her name was Chase. I wanted to be with her – in a young boy's way – more than anything in the world. But I wasn't anywhere near in her league. Well, at least I didn't think so. But when I was home, I would stare at the telephone for hours. I was trying to will Chase to call me."

"And, did she call?"

"No. It's stupid to think that you can will someone to call – or come."

"And you're telling me this because?"

"Because while I should have given up juvenile thoughts, I put the key under the mat two days ago, and every time I thought about it, I was hoping against hope that you would be the one to use it," he said.

"Oh. I wonder what that says about seemingly juvenile thoughts. Maybe you've honed your skills. Maybe the receiver had to be –"

"Vulnerable?"

"I was going to say – receptive. Perhaps Chase wasn't receptive." She walked across the dark entryway. Her arm was extended, and when it contacted him, she ran her hand on his chest. She stepped close until their bodies touched. When her fingers moved across his nipple, she felt a slight tremor. She undid the top button of his shirt, and ran her fingers over his bare skin.

"Um, I'm not sure that is a good idea."

"Yes, I know," she said undoing the second button, gaining more access.

"No. Really. There are regulations. You're an officer and – and,"

"Do you feel like I'm taking advantage of my rank – or forcing myself on you?"

"No, ma'am."

"You can stop the ma'am stuff. Besides, what did you think would happen when you put the key under the mat and used your supernatural powers to summon me?"

She unbuttoned the last button on his shirt and spread the garment. She kissed his nipple and felt him quiver. There was the faint fragrance of the soap he'd used, and a saltiness when she licked his skin. Another quiver. She was feeling warmth spreading through her. Her stomach fluttered. She kissed his nipple, opening her lips, sucking it into her mouth. He jerked. She lifted her chin and felt his lips on her neck. Soft butterfly kisses, along with longer, powerful ones. Their mouths crushed against each other. Lips parted. Her tongue pushed into his mouth, probing, searching. She felt his tongue pushing back. Their breaths were rapid and shallow. She could feel his on her face, and his chest rising and falling rapidly. Her hands found his belt, pulling frantically to get it undone.

He pulled back and looked at her. Everything stopped. *He looks sad. No. He knows if we do this, there's no undoing it. And what happens then –* She kissed him, pushed her tongue into his mouth, then undid the belt completely. She pulled the trouser button apart and yanked on the sides to open the zipper. Putting her hands on his sides, she slid his trousers and underwear to his ankles. On her knees, she pulled his legs up, one at a time, until he stood essentially naked before her. His cock was fully engorged. She placed her hand on it and grasped it, sliding her hand back and forth while caressing his scrotum softly with her other hand.

"I – uh – you might be – uh – careful – it's been a long time –"

He pulled her up and crushed his mouth against hers. She was lifted off the ground and into his arms in one smooth movement. He carried her into the bedroom.

She felt him lay her carefully on the bed as he softly kissed her neck. She dropped her head back to open herself to him. He kissed her neck and moved slowly toward her chest. She pulled on her blouse, ripping the first three buttons open. His mouth placed soft, lingering kisses on her chest. With each one placed, coolness lingered from the moisture of his lips.

He unfastened the front fastener of her bra and pulled the sides away, exposing her nipples and making them stiffen. He kissed each slowly – first so softly that she hardly knew he was there. Then, he carefully sucked each between his lips and massaged each with his tongue as he did so. Her stomach contracted and she shook. Heat and energy built within her.

His lips were on her stomach. Lower. Now her abdomen. The top of her shorts parted, the zipper opened, and they slid down her legs, off into oblivion. Only her thong remained. Her hands were shaking, but she moved them to pull the thong off. She felt her hands in his. *Nooo. Let me – I want it off. I want you in me. Now!* His tongue traced the band. Her desire was fast building to where she wouldn't be able to control her movements. Her legs were moving on their own. Her hands pulled to be free of his. His tongue was on her inner thighs, then she felt it on her clit – through the thong. She fought to free her hands and pull the thong away.

He continued his maddeningly slow attack. His tongue slid under the fabric, and she felt it touch her. "Oh! God! Yes!" His tongue played across her. She was heating beyond return. Her heart was pounding. An electric current pulsed through her, growing every second. She was wet, very wet. Her stomach contracted. She wanted her hands free to grab and pull. He released her hands and grabbed the thong by the sides, sliding it free of her – kissing the sides of her derriere as it moved to her knees.

She kicked her legs, engaging the garment with one foot and finally pushing it free of her. She spread her legs wide apart. "Now." It was a quiet plea, almost begging to be free of the sexual fire that tormented her. His lips touched her clitoris. He opened his mouth and sucked her into him, lashing her captured bud with his tongue. Dee exploded. Her back arched, legs curled, arms pulled against her. Still, the sucking and licking continued. She was shaking – beyond control. Finally, it was overwhelming. She was too sensitive. She started pushing him away, pulling herself back from his mouth – which had given so much pleasure, now each touch made her jump from excessive sensitivity.

"Oh! God! Oh! God! You can stop now! Please! Stop now!" The torment finally stopped. Strong hands massaged her legs. Occasional aftershocks occurred.

"You okay?"

"I'm not sure. Is this heaven?"

"California."

"Close enough. I think I saw heaven. I thought I was going through hell to get there. You really made me wait."

"Complaining?"

"Not now. Half the fun may be in getting there, but the reward is in a great arrival. Give me a few minutes to recover, and we'll do something for you."

His arms engulfed her. She slid her naked body against his, exhaled and relaxed into a contented state of bliss.

Forty-two

Dee opened her eyes. The red numbers on the clock read 12:07. Arms engulfed her. She moved back against him, her bottom connecting with his shaft. It began to enlarge.

"Are you awake? It would seem part of you is for sure. Ready for action at the touch of a – um – bottom?"

"And such a cute little bottom it is, too."

"I'm not so sure about the cute or the little."

"I am. And very distracting. Even in those tailored uniform slacks."

"Chief Petty Officer Jackson! Have you been watching an officer's behind?"

"Not just any officer. Just one. And it's more like ogling than watching. Surreptitiously. Besides, it's my duty to watch you. Nothing in the regs says I can't enjoy the view. I wasn't *just* watching your booty."

"I think using the word 'just' gave you away."

"In the words of Jimmy Carter, 'I've lusted in my heart.' Will I be punished?"

"You'll have to endure hours of hard labor." With that, she turned and faced him, kissing him as she grasped his cock in her hand. "Let's see where we can confine this unruly member." She giggled and rolled him on his back, then straddled him.

They kissed. Slowly and softly. Then, she pulled condom number two from the package and slowly rolled it down his shaft.

He moaned. "You're doing that slowly just to tease me, aren't you?"

"Half the fun of the trip is the journey. I'd hate to arrive at the destination too soon," she said with a smile. She crawled up his body, her knees on either side of him, and slowly sat so that he entered her slightly. Then, she straightened and caused him to withdraw almost completely. She repeated this over and over until he was finally completely within her. "See. Wasn't that worth the wait?"

"Oh my god! You're going to kill me."

"You seemed to like making me wait earlier. I just thought what was good for me would be good for you, as well. Not so?"

"Please!" He started to move under her, thrusting faster than she was moving.

"Stop that! I'll be the one who decides how soon."

"I'm not sure –"

"Oh, yes you can." She leaned forward and held his wrists down firmly in her hands. She began to move with slow, deliberate thrusts of her hips. When his breathing became fast and irregular, she stopped completely. "There, now. We'll just rest awhile." And she started to kiss and nip at his nipples.

"You're torturing me!"

"Well, maybe sweet torture," with another nip he jumped, "I think you're complaining when you should just be enjoying this. I won't take too long with my fun – maybe an hour," she said sweetly. "Or so." He moaned and she kissed him. Then she started slowly riding his shaft, feeling him fill her completely. *I want him to explode inside me as much as he does, but then, where would the fun be in that?*

His breathing was heavier and he was moving under her, trying to thrust harder and faster. She stopped moving then slowly slid him out of her completely. "You need to play by my rules. I could keep this up all night." *No, I can't. I almost came myself.* When he had settled slightly, she reinserted him and pushed down on him to engulf him completely. *Oh god! That feels sooooo good.*

Three more times, she brought him to the edge, and then pulled him back. Each time it was more difficult – for her as well as him. Finally, he could contain himself no longer. His back arched and he lifted her off the bed, burying himself even deeper within her. With a gasp, she began to shake violently, barely aware that he was shaking uncontrollably under her. Her insides exploded, sending shockwave after shockwave from deep within her center to her fingers and toes. Her limbs became useless and she collapsed on his chest, shaking, shaking. Or was it him? She didn't know. She didn't care. She'd never tormented anyone like she had him and she'd never had the explosive orgasm that resulted.

Forty-three

They lay naked under the covers. They were snuggled together, Dee's back against his front, her legs were pulled up and bent at the knees. His legs fitting against hers perfectly. Both were lost in half sleep, totally relaxed and worn out from a night of bliss.

"We've almost used up your condoms," she said. "Two of the three. And why only three, anyway?"

Why only three, indeed. "After my divorce, let's just say I wasn't interested in – uh – relationships. Originally, my good friends got me one. They said it was a lifetime supply. Ayala replaced it with three. He said he wanted me to have one to use, should the occasion, um, come up –"

She giggled.

"and have two for water balloons, or something."

"Well, I'm glad you didn't use the other two for water balloons." She was laughing.

"Yeah. Me too."

"So, if we use the last one, what happens? Is that it?"

"It was supposed to be a lifetime supply, so I have to stop doing – this – I have to get more, or it's the end of my life."

"Why don't we say it's the start of your next life? Besides, while you may not know this, there are stores, here. We can always get more."

"I do like that idea best," and he kissed her softly on the back of the neck.

She snuggled against him. "It's what you deserve." She was quiet for a moment, then almost at a whisper, "I wonder what I deserve."

What do you deserve? You deserve to be held close when you need comfort, warmth or security. To be free when you don't. You deserve someone strong enough to there for you, to be your equal partner in life. You deserve someone who will trust you so completely, they will hand you their power and serve your every need. Someone who will cherish you. Someone who will worship you.

"You deserve all the good and wonderful things in life," he said aloud, and with that, he pulled her even closer. She wiggled her bottom against him and he felt a now familiar enlargement.

"I guess we're going to find out what happens when we use the last one. I'm betting on a next – and better – life." With that, she reached up and grabbed the last of the condoms, ripped it open and pulled it out. "Third time's the charm – although the first two were pretty charming, too."

Forty-four

He stood at the picture window in the living room looking out at the ocean. The sun was up, playing on the sea through clouds which were sprinkled across the morning sky. He sipped his coffee and thought of the night before. It had been a great night, and he was filled with emotions he hadn't felt in a long time. Joy. Elation. Satisfaction. Adoration. Confusion. And unease. He was trying to deny the last, but it remained.

Incredible. Only word to describe it. I'm glad I haven't forgotten how – it's been a long time. I guess it is like riding a bicycle. Well, not quite. Exhausting, but much more fun. But now. It's forbidden. There's got to be some way.

The door behind him opened and she emerged from the bedroom, wearing the too big white terry robe.

"Good morning."

"Good morning to you, too," she said as she walked to the counter where the coffee maker was. She poured a cup and smiled when she noted there were two French vanilla creamers and a pack of Splenda next to the cup. She added them and kept turned away from him.

"We – we need to – I mean last night was maybe the most wonderful night of my life, but –"

He put his arms around her, his hands on her stomach. He felt her melt slightly. He turned her toward him, his hands now on her lower back. He leaned down and kissed her softly, and he felt her melt into his body.

"We need to – really – I thought we could – and it would be fine. But now –" She was searching for words.

He lifted her gently and sat her on the counter. He stepped closer. Her knees parted and he pushed against her.

"Look, I'm trying to sort some things out. You know as well as I do that –"

He pulled at the single overhand knot on the robe tie, undoing it and at the same time parting the robe revealing her naked body within. Desire stirred within him.

"That's not helping the situation. Sooner or later –"

He touched the nipple of her left breast, first softly with his lips, then with his tongue. It stiffened immediately. He continued down her body. On one knee, he kissed her clit, softly, slowly. Her legs parted more, and he ran his tongue the length of her folds.

"Oooo! Okay, I guess we can make it later. Don't let me fall off the counter."

"Just lean back and enjoy," he said as he returned to his ministrations. Something more than desire and lust surged within him. Reverence. This wonderful woman allowing him to pleasure her. Beautiful, smart; he wasn't sure he was worthy, but he was going to do his best to take her to ecstasy. His tongue pushed inside her. He felt her legs jerk, then quiver. He could taste her as she responded and he worked his tongue harder. In. Out.

Around. He found her growing and hardening clit and concentrated on that, licking faster and faster, until he felt her legs start to shake. Then, he sucked every bit of her labia into his mouth increasing and relaxing pressure intermittently while he continued to lick furiously. He felt her hand on his forehead, gently pushing him away, then more forcefully until he released her.

"I thought you were going to kill me there. I'm so out of" – she took a couple of deep breaths – "sex shape." Then, her hands on either side of his face she pulled him up and kissed him.

"You okay?"

"I'm not sure. I'm not sure I can still walk," she laughed.

"Well, then," he said, and before she could object, he lifted her from the counter, carried her to the couch and set her down. Then, he retrieved her coffee and his before sitting down himself.

"But wait, we didn't do anything for you."

"Trust me, you did plenty for me."

"I mean now, er, just then."

"I repeat my earlier statement, I enjoyed it as much as you did."

"I doubt that," she giggled. Then, more seriously, "We still have to talk, you know."

He was quiet.

"Cat got your tongue?"

"Well, at least you didn't use the P word," he said smiling.

She laughed, almost spilling coffee out her nose. "Not fair. I'll have to find a way to get you back, you know."

"I look forward to it." Then a pause. "I know we've got to find some way. I – my past. I didn't think anyone would ever – I haven't dated. I wasn't interested. Then, I met you. There was something about you – from the first. Defiant little woman struggling with the tire. I knew who you were. You should have seen your face when I came into your office. I had a hard time not breaking up. But there was always something about you."

"What made you think anyone wouldn't be interested in you? You're a great guy. I'm sure there are a lot of women who would want to be with you."

"It's not that. I just don't want to be with them."

He saw her looking at him as if she was trying to understand.

"My wife – ex-wife. We were married three and a half years. During my drug interdiction days. I spent a fair amount of time at sea. As it turns out, while I was out riding the waves, she was riding anything that would look at her."

"Oh, my god!"

"Yeah. I finally got wise, well, she got careless. So, next time I went out, I had somebody watch. When I got confirmation, I confronted her. First, she denied it. Then tried to tell me it was only that one time. Finally, she relented and said we should get a divorce, but she wanted it to be 'amicable.' I agreed, and we were going to stay in the same house until she could find a place. She made me lunch and I went off to work. She'd included a thermos of coffee, but it tasted 'off' to me. So, I had it tested. Ethylene glycol. Antifreeze. A lot of people have used it as a poison over many years. Almost undetectable. Until they started adding a bitter chemical to it – you know, to stop people from using it as a poison."

"Oh, my god! That's the worst thing I ever heard."

"Well, long story short – well – shorter, the police were able to catch her trying it again, and not only did I get the divorce, she didn't have to look for a place to live. The state provided one – for four and a half years. Time off for good behavior and all."

She set down her coffee and hugged him. "I can't believe what she did – what you've been through."

"Yeah, well, now you understand why I've been 'off' dating."

"Yes, and – oh no! That day on the boat. I said something and you got quiet – mad maybe. I said something about having to get rid of someone after you're done with them. I'm sorry. I didn't know."

"Very few know – unless you were one of those who knew me back then. Ayala knows. We worked together."

"That's terrible. Not Ayala. That someone would try to poison you. What did she think she would get?"

"I don't know. Insurance maybe. Probably the furniture. Maybe sympathy as a grieving widow instead of the woman divorced for sleeping with the entire county."

"Grieving black widow."

He kissed her. "Water under the bridge. Right now, because you broke the spell of the evil queen, we have a problem to figure out."

Forty-five

Dee sat at her desk. She'd piled file folders filled with assorted papers on her desk in an effort to look busy. She was lost in confusion. What she wanted. What she felt. What she feared. And, what she might have lost. It was one of the greatest nights of her life. At the same time, it was terrifying. It could mean the end of her career. She wanted two mutually exclusive things.

She might have turned the lights out in an effort to hide, but that would just draw more attention.

The door opened and Annie came in.

"Uh, I'm really busy today. I don't have time for –."

"Please. I've worked here for ten years and know when every report, every deadline, and every meeting is. There isn't anything –" She closed the door, then fell back against it, her eyes and mouth wide open. "Oh My God! You did it!"

Dee's head snapped up in panic. Her face was getting red. "What are you talking about? I didn't do anything." She was trying to remain calm. Is something tattooed on my forehead?

"No. You did it. I know."

"I didn't do anything. I don't know what you think you know."

Annie slid into a chair. For a moment, she just stared at Dee.

"What are you —"

"Shush!" She sat for a moment or two longer, a satisfied smile on her face.

"I asked what you were doing."

Annie sat back in her chair, studied the ceiling for a minute, then looked her in the eyes. "Okay. Not many people know this, and you've got to keep it secret. Got it?"

Dee just stared.

"I've got a super power."

Dee's face dropped in disbelief.

"No. Really. Even people who know don't believe me. I've got sex-dar."

"What?"

"Sex-dar. It's like radar, but for sex."

"That's not a thing."

"Yuh huh! How else would I know you got, um, let's be gentile about it and say nailed? Yeah. Nailed. By the way, where is he?" Annie started looking around, as if she would find him hiding in the office.

"Who?" asked Dee.

"Are you still going to play *that* game? Scott. I know headquarters allowed him back after the testimony was done. Saw the order. Anyway, I'd say 'the chief,' but since you two have been intimate, 'the chief' seems a bit formal. By the way, the more vigorous the intimacy, the stronger I feel it. Man, you guys must have really had a good time. Make that GREAT time."

"Again, nothing happened. And, I believe Chief Jackson came in early and took a boat out – something about checking on maintenance he'd done."

"Oh! So now we're back to Chief Jackson, are we? Chicken. Ooo! I'll be right back." She rushed out the door, returning in a few minutes with a mug of coffee.

"Really. I should –"

"Pu-lease. You've got nothing to do. I'm going to wait for the flowers."

"Flowers?"

"Yeah. Good guys always send flowers. And, he's a good guy. My guess is roses. Red. Probably a dozen. He'd like to send more, but too many, you know like three dozen, just draws undue attention. It's like 'ding, ding, ding, something really important happened to this lady. Or with this lady. Or in this lady.' So, I'm going with a dozen. Red. Long stem. High quality. Oh yeah." She slapped a ten-dollar bill on Dee's desk. "Ten dollars says there's no card. Ante up." Annie sat back in her chair, a smug look on her face, and nodded at the bill on the desk.

"This is ridiculous," said Dee as she reached into her purse and put ten dollars on top on Annie's. "I tell you, nothing happened."

"Honey, we just placed a bet on whether there will be a card with the flowers. The ship has sailed on any denials. Don't commit any crimes. The cops will bust you in no time flat. Probably before you have time to get home or hide the loot."

She sagged and started to cry. After a few minutes, she composed herself. "Okay. I'll admit it. You guessed. And for us, it is a crime."

"I didn't guess. I knew. I told you I have sex-dar."

"I don't believe you, but if I did, believe you, that is, when did you – um – realize you had this – uh – gift."

"I didn't know what it was for a long time." Annie looked up as if trying to remember a long-lost memory. "I've had it most of my life, I guess. I noticed something strange when I'd come home from elementary school and Uncle George was there with my mom. Something was off. Then, in middle school, I got weird vibes from some of the kids – and teachers – not together. I can tell that, too. It's different if it's 'wrong,' like rape, incest, or with children. Self-satisfaction, if you get my drift, comes to me differently, too. They say I'll probably lose my gift once I'm no longer a virgin."

Dee stared at her with her mouth open.

"Really? You believe that? I'd have lost it first year in high school. That's kind of how I figured it out. I get that open stare a lot from the few I've told. Most try to avoid me afterwards. I guess they're embarrassed when I know when they got lucky – or when they were playing solitaire instead." She took a sip of her coffee.

"Um, not that I'm anxious to hear the answer, but what happens when you –"

"Oh, yeah. Kind of blows the whole thing away for a few days. Overload, I guess. Like getting a flashbulb popped in your eyes in a dark room. Huh. Popped." She looked at the ceiling, a faraway look in her eyes.

"And you know – how?"

Annie returned her attention to the here and now. "Pheromones, or something. I'm not even sure. It's been so long; I didn't recognize it at first. But, MAN, it hit like a ton of bricks when I came in here. Nice to know I haven't lost it. You must have had a doozy of a night. Of course, I went to Catholic school. We couldn't talk about having sex. So, instead, we'd talk about gingersnap cookies. You know, 'Billy Johnson and I just had the greatest gingersnap cookie behind the football field bleachers.' Teachers never caught on. A couple even baked gingersnaps for parties. I found out Billy Johnson had a lot of gingersnap cookies behind those bleachers. Surprised he didn't shrivel up. Of course,"

There was a knock on the door. Petty Officer Swanson stuck her head in. "Uh, delivery for you, lieutenant."

A man entered carrying a vase that appeared to hold a dozen red roses. Dee tried her best to look normal.

Annie took the vase and set it on the corner of the desk. "Oh. Excuse me, sir. There doesn't seem to be a card." She turned and smiled at Dee. "Do you have who they were sent by?"

The delivery man opened a sheet of paper. "Uh, yeah, Templar, Simon Templar. Three Miracle Way, Victorville."

Annie thanked the man, tipped him the twenty dollars from the corner of the desk, and plopped into the chair. "Could have been more creative. Simon Templar – you know, The Saint. Val Kilmer did okay in the 1997 movie.

Roger Moore did a TV series in the 60s. George Sanders did a great job in the 1940s series. Bet he wasn't a saint last night. Not George Sanders. He's dead. I mean Scott. By the way, it takes three miracles to become a Catholic saint. Three Miracle Way was a nice touch. Three miracles. Makes me wonder how many times – not that you'd tell me."

"Please. Please. Please don't say anything to anybody. This is a career ender. I don't know what to do."

"Oh, come now." Annie smiled sweetly, paused, then said, "Too soon? Don't worry. I never tell. Well, not quite true. In college, there was one of the girls – she was nice. I liked her – as a friend. I could tell the guy she was dating was getting some, on the side, if you catch my drift. She wasn't at the same time he was. I told her I thought I'd seen him with someone else. She investigated and caught him. You? You're a friend, too. I wouldn't do anything to hurt you or your career. Maybe we can figure a way."

"If you can, it will be a fourth miracle."

"Well, I'm guessing the magic number was three then."

Dee sat back, deflated and resigned. "By the way, I found out about the wife."

"Do tell. Wait. We'll do lunch. Someplace private where you can give me all the details. Maybe some about last night, as well. We can walk up the street."

"It may have to wait. I barely made it in this morning. I'm having trouble moving. Sore. All over. There. Happy?"

"Wow! I didn't have to drag it out of you. So, give. Why no women?"

"Well, his former wife had a fidelity problem."

Annie stared at her.

"From what he said, she did pretty much any guy who was able. Maybe some who were only borderline able. He found out and confronted her. She fought the divorce thing at first, then said okay. Made him some coffee – laced with antifreeze. She got caught and sent up the river for almost five years. Doesn't seem long enough for attempted murder. Why would you do such a thing?"

Annie's eyes narrowed. "Maybe money."

"Money? How much money? He's a chief. Even if he saved most of it, and with life insurance, how much could there be?"

"He's got money somewhere. Either that or he's a thief. I assume you were in his bedroom. I peeked in during a couple of the parties I was invited to. With the enlisted. Actually lay on his bed for a couple of minutes – thinking about what it might be like. Maybe you weren't looking around when you were there. Otherwise occupied I would assume. Concentrating on something else, perhaps? That picture on the wall? The pond."

"Yeah. Copy of a – Renoir, I think. Saw it in art appreciation class. Renoir did a number of them."

"Yeah. Not a copy. Real thing."

"No. That's impossible. If it were real, it would be worth – worth –"

"Killing a man for?"

"Yeah," she said quietly. "I'm really glad we didn't squirt anything on it."

Annie's eyes opened wide. "You know, there isn't anything you could say right now that would surprise me."

"Ten dollars?"

"Sure."

"He didn't make me sleep in the wet spot." And she stuck her tongue out.

"Shit." Annie laughed, then reached into her pocket and put ten dollars on the desk.

Forty-six

Scott sat on the stern of the response boat, water dripping off his body. His SCUBA gear sat on the deck behind him. The boat rocked gently on the swells. Ayala sat across from him; his gear next to Scott's. A 'Diver Down' flag floated near the boat.

"So," said Ayala, "*what* are we doing out here?"

"Maintenance check."

"Uh, what are we checking?"

"How about ship's hull integrity? That make you happy?"

"Ship's hull integrity? This boat's been in the water for four days. The bilge is dry as a bone."

"Guess the maintenance worked."

Ayala was quiet for a minute. "How long we known each other?"

Scott looked at him. "What – twelve, yeah, twelve years. A little more. Why?"

"Yeah. We were on that drug interdiction together. The day you saved my life."

"God, you were walking around with your head stuck up so high," Scott laughed. "It's like you were saying, 'Shoot me! Shoot me!' then we ran into the scared moron they left on the boat when they bailed."

"You pulled me back just as he pulled the trigger. I just about peed myself when I saw the hole in the bulkhead where my head had been." Ayala was shaking his head. "Man, I was glad you were there."

"I don't know whose eyes were bigger – you or the guy who shot." Scott was laughing.

"I've been with you ever since. Transfer for transfer."

"Yeah. Good to have you – shipmate."

"Nobody knows you better than I do."

Scott was quiet.

"So, what's going on?"

"Nothing's going on. Maybe I just wanted some time to myself."

"Then, why'd you bring me?"

"Kind of wondering myself now that you ask."

"Something's bothering you. You're different."

"Maybe I'm thinking about retirement and what I'll do."

"We both know what you'll do," said Ayala. "Family business. No. This is different. I've only seen you this way once before."

"Tread carefully."

"It was because of her. That's when you got – let's call it this way."

"I'm not 'this way,' as you say."

"No? But my guess is that the general cause is the same."

"You're off base and getting into an area that you shouldn't be getting into."

"After her, you locked your heart away. I understand. Guys aren't supposed to talk like that, but we're closer – I care about you. Nobody's gotten near you since then. Not that they haven't tried. You're pretty good at deflecting them. Something's changed."

Scott was staring at the California shoreline about a mile away.

"You know," Ayala continued, "it's funny. You're working along. In today's world, men and women working together. Doing the same or similar jobs. Sometimes you're co-workers. Sometimes you're the boss. Sometimes they are. You get along with some more than others. Then, maybe you find you're getting along with one better than others. You find your days are better when you're working with that person. Then, maybe you realize the days are better when that person is at work that day, and not as good when they aren't. You enjoy their company. Just knowing they are there. Maybe there's a warmth. Then, one day you realize that you've fallen in love. Hits you like a shovel in the back of the head."

"I don't have any idea what you're even talking about."

"Just thinking out loud. But I saw the way you were looking at the L T. It wasn't, 'Oh, I'd really like to jump on that.' And it wasn't, 'Gee, what a lovely woman.' Something else was going on. Lately, she's been looking at you the same way. My guess is that one or both of you are trying to figure out what to do about it."

"You couldn't be further from the truth."

"I'm sure. I just wanted you to know, if you need anything – anything at all, legal or illegal, not that you'd want anything illegal, I'm here."

"I guess we've checked the maintenance long enough."

"Yeah, gee. By the time we get back, the watch should be set. Anybody you're hoping to avoid? Swanson will be crushed."

"What? Who?"

"Swanson. I think she was planning an assault on the monk of Sandy Point."

"The little twenty-three-year-old?"

"Yeah. The little twenty-three-year-old with the killer body. Nice girl, too. With any luck, I can get her on the rebound."

"Jesus. Get the anchor."

Forty-seven

Dee sat on her couch, arms across her chest, and her legs pulled up. An untouched glass of wine sat on the coffee table in front of her. Caddy corner across sat Annie in one of the facing armchairs. Pink fuzzy sweater, pale blue pedal-pushers, and bare feet. She was on her second glass.

"Growing up," started Dee, "we had what I guess is the normal family unit – or was – if there ever was one. Normal family unit. My dad worked, and my mom stayed home. My dad was a good provider. My mom took good care of us."

"Sounds pretty nice to me," said Annie.

"Yeah, but all my mom ever got to do was laundry, cleaning, and anything in the kitchen. I mean, she had time for us, too, but that was her life."

"Sounds like a good mother."

"Yes, she was, but I sometimes got the feeling that she had dreams beyond just being a good mother and wife. She never said, but I could see the sadness sometimes."

Annie sipped her wine and let her think for a bit.

"And my dad – as far as he was concerned, that was what a woman was for. Women's work. The few times I tried to do something he considered as a man's job, he'd chase me off. Saying something like, 'that's for a man to do. Girls need to stick to girly things.' Or, he'd set me up to fail. Probably so I'd be satisfied with his version of a woman's life. But he made me more nervous about doing what I wanted. He succeeded in making me - cautious. Overly afraid of failing. Part of the reason I had trouble with the flat tire. And Scott had to do the garbage disposal. I wouldn't have known where to start."

"You're being harder on yourself than you should be," said Annie. "Lots of people – men and women – can't change a flat. That's why the auto club is so popular. And almost nobody knows how to do a garbage disposal."

"Well, I decided that I wasn't going to live like that. I wanted to go out and do something. Something more than laundry, cleaning, and cooking. Sometimes I think I did it as much for my mom as for myself."

"There's nothing wrong with that."

"My dad was upset that I headed off to college. Thought it was a waste of time and money. After all, he thought I was going to get married and do exactly what my mom was doing. You don't need a college degree for that. So, when I got to college, I had to work to put myself through. My mom sent money when she could. Every penny helped. I was looking for ways to pay the bills, when the Coast Guard came along. Pay for me to finish school, and an advanced degree down the road. The answer to my prayers."

"I'm glad you did. It's nice knowing you," Annie said as she raised her wine glass in salute.

"Thank you. You, too. But my career became the most important thing in my life. I was going to show my dad that I could be more than a servant for some man."

"Hence, turning down a great life in the Hamptons."

"Just a more luxurious prison. I was doing fine."

"Until – maybe – you found out that the career was peppered with more hazards than you thought. And, somebody who helped you with some of the hazards got a hook into your heart."

"I discovered that I want both. And I can't have both. I love my mom, but I don't want her life. I want my career, but I'm starting to think I want more than that, as well. And no matter how much I try to figure a way out, I just get more confused. It's one or the other."

"There's got to be a way around all or none – or one or the other."

"Well, when the inquiry is over, I may not have a career. With the way things are going he may not want me either."

Forty-eight

Dee stood outside the room where the last day of the inquiry would take place. Officers and civilians stood in small groups. There was the undertone of hushed conversation. She looked at her watch. 9:12. Eighteen minutes until the proceedings would begin. A flock of birds were fighting insider her. Her hands were trembling. Her whole career might hang in the balance.

She saw him walking toward her, the heels of his shoes sounding on the marble floor. He was wearing the short-sleeved summer uniform, which fit him perfectly. The left side of his chest was covered with ribbons. Shirt and trousers sharply creased. Tan muscular arms extending from the sleeves. *God! He looks like a living recruiting poster!* A smile curled slightly at the corners of her mouth. Those birds stopped fighting. Maybe they were distracted by the tingling feeling that grew within her.

He walked directly to her. "Good morning, lieutenant." It seemed overly formal. Perhaps it was the day.

"Good morning."

"Could we talk? Privately?" He motioned to the colonnade balcony to her left.

"Certainly."

They walked to the balcony in silence. There was a spectacular view of the Pacific Ocean in the distance. A cool breeze met them as they walked to the marble railing. He removed his combination cover and placed it under his left arm.

"Beautiful, isn't it?" he said as he faced the railing and looked at the sea beyond.

"Yes, it is," she said. He seemed distant. "Is there something —"

"No matter what happens today, you'll be okay. You should know that."

"I don't under —"

"Worst case scenario — even if you receive a letter of reprimand, that won't end your career. Maybe slow you a bit, but you'll still do okay."

She looked at him, but he was staring at the ocean. His face like stone.

"It's funny," he said. "You don't even know how it happens. You meet someone. They are attractive. That part doesn't really matter. But there are rules. You have a professional relationship. You find out they are smart, effective, dedicated. They earn your respect. Then, you discover that your day seems brighter when they are there, darker when they aren't. You smile more when they are around. One day, you wake up and know you're in love. Or, you're working together one day and your eyes meet theirs. There's a feeling in your heart and soul. Life becomes wonderful and hopeless at the same time. Maybe you try to deny it, but in your heart of hearts, you know the truth." He took a deep breath.

"I love you," he said.

"I love you, too," she said.

"The problem is, the service doesn't recognize love. They forbid it when the people who find themselves in love are from different classes."

"Classes?"

"Officer. Enlisted. Love becomes a crime punishable through court martial by dishonorable discharge. In rare cases, brig time. Used to be the officer would bear the brunt, but now both careers would be over. I can't let that happen. You've worked hard to get where you are now and for your chance of promotion and great things in your future. But the truth is, the service deserves and needs good officers, and you're a good officer."

"Are you – are you –" The birds in her stomach were threatening to fly out her mouth. *Oh, god! Please don't throw up!*

"I've requested an immediate transfer. I can't trust myself to not do something that would betray you. Every time I see you, I want to hold you. I want to kiss you."

She turned away from him. Her eyes filled with water. Her insides were hollow.

"You know," he continued, "that I was married once. Years ago. She betrayed me. I ran away – hid. Out of anger and fear. I'm leaving now not out of fear. I'm leaving because I love you so much that I can't trust myself not to show it. And showing how I feel would ruin everything you've worked for and want. Just remember that I love you."

She took a deep breath and slowly released it. It took a full minute to compose herself. "Isn't there some way –" she said as she turned toward him. But there was nobody there. She sucked in her breath and began crying. It was a few minutes later that a voice behind her announced, "We're getting ready to start, lieutenant." She wiped the tears from her face and started toward the meeting room.

Forty-nine

She sat at the table, barely listening to the recitation of the evidence presented in the inquiry. A few experts were called. She perked up a bit when she heard Trahir say, "According to the sworn, written testimony of Chief Jackson, the attack took place in an unexpected and rapid manner that did not allow for preparation or response. Whether that is the finding of this inquiry remains to be seen." After a bit of paper shuffling, "Are there any other individuals who can provide material information to this inquiry? Hearing none, I adjourn this meeting for today. I will present my findings on Monday morning at 10 AM."

The room emptied. Dee stood and headed for the powder room adjoining, feeling like an automaton – leaden arms and legs moving without purpose. She set her purse on the counter and looked into the mirror, trying to judge just how bad her makeup looked. For as bad as she felt, her makeup didn't seem to betray her. The powder room door closed behind her. She turned, expecting to see another woman. Instead, it was Captain Trahir.

"What are you doing in here?"

"I just thought I would check up on you."

"Why?"

"You're in a tough spot, lieutenant. The evidence could go either way. Doesn't look good. Should I do you a favor — or not? My decision will stand — and be respected. Your future is in my hands. You need to make sure I am in a good humor when I review the evidence — when I decide what the evidence shows — dereliction of duty, or otherwise."

"And to ensure your — good humor?"

"I will need to see you this evening. Your apartment will suffice. We can discuss the pertinent information and — you will likely need to convince me — somehow, that your actions were in keeping with service expectations. I expect this will be done with a cheerful attitude. Do I make myself clear?"

Her stomach churned and the heat of anger filled her. She couldn't believe what she was hearing.

"I said, do I make myself clear?" His tone was rough and menacing.

"Perfectly."

"Then, I'll see you at eight o'clock." He turned and left the powder room, closing the door behind him.

Dee turned and looked into the mirror. Tears were running down her face, her mascara making trails as they descended. The day had started so differently — a woman in love with a dubious but a hopefully bright future. Now, Scott was gone and her future was in jeopardy — depending on how well she could 'perform' for that bastard Trahir.

Fifty

Dee was sitting at her counter, dressed in jeans and a sweatshirt. Her hands were shaking and wet with perspiration. She'd worked hard to get where she was, now, her career was going to depend on – on prostitution. It was 8:12 when there was a knock on the door. She jumped. She willed herself to go to the door and pull it open. Trahir was on the other side. His face showed the look of smug victory. She wanted to throw up.

She turned and walked back to the kitchen. The door closed.

"That's not a very cordial welcome."

"I'm having trouble with this."

"Yes, I thought you might. Do you have some wine?"

Dee opened a bottle of wine. She poured some into each of two glasses. She set them on the counter and pushed one toward him.

"Oh, it's not for me. I won't be drinking wine. You will." He pulled a bottle from his coat. He opened the bottle and poured a small amount of liquid into her wine glass. "I knew you might have – misgivings – so I've decided to make sure those don't interfere with the evening."

"What is that?"

"Just a little potion to make sure you are, let's say, compliant. You know, in the old days, women knew their place."

"Their place?"

"Yes. The service is a man's world. Women were tolerated, even welcomed. But they understood that the 'extra duties' were what got them to where they wanted to be. Now. Just drink your wine. In a short time, you won't really much care what happens, and I won't have to put up with your – misgivings."

"So, no romantic interlude?"

"Oh, the time for romantic interludes is long gone. Tonight, it's going to be raw sex. Things a proper girl like you wouldn't do under normal circumstances I'm sure. You'll remember just enough." A cruel smile was on his face. "You'll be sore tomorrow, maybe more than just sore. You may feel it still on Monday. But, with any luck, you will have learned your lesson and saved your career. Now. Drink the damn wine."

Dee picked up the wine glass and held it to her mouth. Just as the liquid touched her lips, she tilted the glass upright, then threw the wine into Trahir's face. "You bastard! I wouldn't have sex with you if it meant my life! You have cheapened and debased the trust given to you by this country and the service. Get out! Get out!"

"You little bitch. I'll show you." He stepped toward her.

Dee pulled a butcher's knife out of the block on the counter and pointed it at him menacingly.

"You think I can't take that away from you?" he laughed.

"Maybe one," she said, and pulling a second from the block, "but you're not good enough to get two."

Trahir's face was red. "Your career is over. By the time I get done with you, you'll be lucky to get ten years in Leavenworth. You'll rue the day you turned me down." He turned on his heel and headed for the door. As he reached for the knob, he spit in her direction.

Trahir pulled the door open and started out, running into special agent Harvard.

"Why, Captain Trahir. Fancy meeting you here."

"Get out of my way," he said, starting to push past her. A very large African American man appeared behind agent Harvard.

"Maybe you should take your hands off the lady – sir."

Agent Harvard smiled. "Captain Frank Trahir, I am placing you under arrest for the crime of aggravated sexual assault. In addition, you will likely be charged with fraternization and threats against a junior officer. Empty your pockets."

"I will not."

Harvard looked at the large officer, "Tiny?"

The large officer stepped forward.

"Never mind." He started to empty his pockets. He turned and tried to flip the bottle past them into the bushes beyond.

"Really? Did you think that would work? Besides, once we process your clothes, we'll find out what it is. The wine. Remember?"

The officer called 'Tiny' retrieved and handed her the bottle. He had a rubber glove on his hand. She placed it into an evidence bag.

"Gosh, I wonder if this could be a bottle of Rohypnol. If it turns out to be, you can add possession of an illegal drug – and an attempt to drug a junior female officer for the purpose of forced sexual acts. By the way, lieutenant, when you called me at 7:55, you forgot to end the call. I had to listen to all that stuff that happened between you and the," she paused and looked at Trahir with disdain, "captain. Lucky I was coming over here anyway. I'll need you to come down to the office and provide a statement in the morning. Captain. We'll provide you with appropriate accommodations for the evening. I would suggest you engage legal counsel." Agent Harvard left. The officer called 'Tiny' had Trahir by the arm.

Fifty-one

On Tuesday morning, Dee sat in her office, staring at the open metal clamshell box on the desk, and what was inside. She'd just finished telling Annie how the final day of the inquiry had gone. Trahir had not been there. The assembled were told he had been 'detained' and unable to attend. Scott had not attended. A rear admiral had read from a script, stating the official report would be published at a later date. The sinking of the watercraft was determined to be due to the unforeseeable actions of criminals unknown at this time. The crew managed to save themselves only through timely and heroic actions. The inquiry was closed.

Annie sat in a chair on the other side of her desk. "Impressive. I'll bet there aren't many lieutenants who wear a bronze star."

"Yeah. I should be happy with the outcome."

"Yes, you should. You were completely exonerated by the board. The sinking had nothing to do with your actions. AND, to really nail that down, they awarded you this," she pointed to the box, "bronze star. It will be great when you come up for promotion. You should be very happy."

"So, why do I feel like a complete fraud? Maybe because I didn't do anything to win this award. I failed to see the danger. I failed to heed Scott's warning and failed to act. I got clunked on the head and knocked out. He pulled me out of the boat – risking his life, by the way. He towed me to the other boat, did all the checking to make sure it was safe, pulled me aboard, and kept me warm and safe until I awoke and help arrived. Oh, yeah, he also kept me from falling overboard when I was puking my guts out because I didn't heed his warning not to look at the corpse and, thinking I could handle it when I couldn't. I didn't see that anywhere in the citation."

"You're being way too hard on yourself. You were in the same situation as he was. You deserve this."

"You know, this is the first time I ever really doubted whether I should be in this business. Despite," she picked up the medal, "this, and I did nothing to deserve it, I failed him – and the station – by what I didn't do."

"So, maybe this wasn't just for the stuff out there," she gestured toward the sea. "You also had the guts to face that bastard Trahir – face him down. And do it in such a way that he won't continue what he had been doing for some time. If you hadn't, there would be other women, other women who might get raped, or worse. Good women who wouldn't finish out a career in the Coast Guard. Good women whose lives would be ruined. And who could have done something for the service and country. You saved them."

"Well, Agent Harvard talked to me after the inquiry closed. The bottle Trahir had was in fact Rohypnol. So, he's charged with having an illegal medication – drug, whatever it is. She listened in to the exchange we had at my place. Recorded it, in fact, and they got a Rohypnol and wine mixture out of the clothes he was wearing, showing he really planned to drug me at the very least. They also got a warrant for his uniform – from the night he accosted me. Had to get it from the dry cleaners – luckily before they actually cleaned it. They found pepper spray on the sleeve, which collaborates my story about that. They're contacting all the other women who have served – if you'll pardon the expression – under him. She said he may get twenty years. And a dishonorable discharge. In a way, it's really sad. His career and marriage are gone. What a waste."

"Yeah, but he had a choice," said Annie. "He did it to himself. He didn't have to be the complete misogynistic ass he was. He didn't have to prey on junior female officers. He deserves everything he gets – probably more than he's going to get."

She was about to reply when Petty Officer Jones stuck her head in, "Got a call from a boat about eight miles out. We need to check it out. You want to come along?" Pause. "Ma'am?"

Suddenly, she wanted to hide. Her hand reached for the piece of red jasper she kept as a paperweight. It was supposed to protect her from unseen danger. "Uh, I should –," as she diverted her eyes and searched her desk for something that needed to be done. "I'm really not feeling well today. It might not be the best idea."

"Forgive me for saying this, Lieutenant, but I think you need to get back on the horse."

"Horse?"

"Yes, ma'am. In this case the horse is a small water craft and you have developed an, uh, aversion. Understandable, but you need to beat it if you want a career. Just my opinion."

Jonesy was right, of course. If she couldn't beat it, her career was over. If Scott were just here, she'd feel so much more confident. He wouldn't always be, but this one day it would be nice.

Fifty-two

The small response boat pulled out of the harbor and onto the ocean beyond. The sky was sunny, and the swells small. A perfect day for boating, but Dee wasn't focused on the beauty of the day.

The boat bounced in the waves, more than usual, it seemed. Each jolted her. Her arms were weak, and she was glad she was sitting. She didn't know how well her wobbly legs would hold up if she'd had to stand for the ride out. *I should order them to turn around and drop me at the station. I don't want to do this. If I freeze and can't function when they needed me, I will hazard the mission. And these people.*

A second class, Barnes, was at the helm. She was seated to his right. Jonesy was sitting slouched behind her. Another enlisted man, Ayala, was sitting in the stern, an assault rifle close at hand. Ayala's head was bouncing as if he were playing music in his mind. *Everyone else is so relaxed. But they weren't almost killed by drug runners.*

"I think I've got the boat." It was Barnes.

She searched the horizon but couldn't see anything. Her hands were clammy, and she wiped them on her trousers. There was a sound behind her and she jumped. Ayala had slapped a magazine into the rifle and chambered a round. He was standing now, popping a piece of gum into his mouth. The bouncing of the head was gone, and his eyes were hard.

"If it's okay with you, ma'am," it was Jonesy, "Barnes will drop us on the boat and back away. Ayala will keep us covered. We can assess if there's an issue. I know it's overkill, but no use taking chances."

Dee started to speak, but words didn't come out at first. Then, "You and Ayala going aboard?" Her legs were dead weight.

"No ma'am. Us. They'll provide stand-off cover." Then, she had a big grin, "This way, you get to evaluate my performance first-hand."

"Uh, I'm not sure —"

"We can't let these bozos have all the fun." Then, quietly, "You gotta do it. It'll be fine. You'll see."

"Hey, Jonesy," it was Barnes. "I'll do her a 360 first. Then, we can hail. If nothing, we can board. Okay?"

"Sounds good Barnes. Ayala?"

Ayala was standing, holding the rifle. He was staring at the horizon, impassive, but the eyes remained hard. Without looking away from the sailboat, he gave a thumbs up.

Dee looked in the direction he was staring and saw a large sailboat in the distance. The mainsail was down and stowed.

Barnes slowed the response boat and circled the sailboat staying 25 yards away. Ayala was glued to the boat, the rifle at the ready. "Get the name?"

"Yeah. Looks like the Christine Elizabeth — out of Santa Barbara."

The response boat's loudspeaker barked and Dee jumped, "Ahoy the Christine Elizabeth. This is the United States Coast Guard. Is anyone on board? Show yourself." There was no response and Barnes repeated it.

"Looks like you're going on board," he said. He pulled alongside.

"Let's go, Lieutenant," said Jonesy.

"Wherever you go," it was Ayala, "remember where I am. Try not step into my field of fire."

Dee's legs were weak, and her hands wet and shaky, but she unbuckled and when the boat pulled next to the sailboat. *Oh, God, this is really happening. Field of fire! Shit! This is real!* The boats touched. Dee looked at the sailboat. *This is what I trained to do. This is what I wanted.* She looked at the Coast Guard crew around her. *I'm going to be what they deserve.* "Let's go!"

She followed Jonesy onto the deck, forward of the cockpit and the door to the interior. She watched the response boat back away to about 10 yards and position on the right stern quarter.

Jonesy led the way down the port side to the cockpit. It was empty. She motioned for Dee to stay where she was and remain quiet, then stepped into the cockpit and hailed the interior.

"This is the United States Coast Guard. Is anyone in the boat? Can you hear me?" Nothing. Then, "I am entering the cabin. If you can hear me, keep your hands in sight when I enter." Jonesy pulled a pistol and entered the cabin. For what seemed like ten minutes, there was no sound. Then, "It's okay lieutenant. Come on down. Bubble gum."

Bubble gum was the safe word. One more security feature to make sure that bad guys didn't force someone to say it was safe when it really wasn't. Dee entered the cabin slowly. When she could see the interior, she noted it was plush – white overhead, mahogany walls, teak deck. Seating in white leather. There was an ice bucket on the table and a bottle in the ice bucket. Flutes were on the table next to the ice bucket. Jonesy was sitting on a couch sipping a coke. Just when she thought she was dreaming, she saw Scott. He was sitting on the other side of Jonesy, his feet propped on the couch. He was wearing jeans and a sweatshirt – as usual.

"Come on in. Have a seat, please," he said.

"What the –"

"You look terrible. I know you're never supposed to say that to a lady, but really, sit. Take a load off. Relax."

Fear turned to disbelief, then, heat filled her face. "You – you – what? Got us out here on a false mayday? Do you know what could – what I could do?"

"Jonesy," he said, looking at the petty officer, "did you tell the lieutenant that you got a distress call?"

"Uh, no chief. I told her we got a call. I thought it would be a good exercise, so we ran it like an unknown distress call. I must have forgotten to tell her that part."

"Oh, my GOD! YOU may be up for a court martial. I've got to tell them," she gestured out of the cabin, "that we aren't in any danger." She turned and stomped up the stairs. When her shoulders were out of the cabin, she looked for the response boat. It was about ten yards away. Ayala was laying on the stern, his shirt off and trousers rolled up. The rifle was locked in its rack. His eyes were closed and his head again was bouncing like he had music playing. Barnes was leaning against the side, behind the wheel, his eyes appeared to be closed.

Dee returned to the interior. "Did everyone know this was a false alarm but me?" she asked harshly.

"Okay, maybe you feel like you've been tricked." It was Jonesy.

Dee just stared.

"Okay, you've been tricked. We knew it was completely safe. You didn't. You needed to prove to yourself – that you still have it. We knew it, but we had to prove it to you. We got you to do it in a way you were safe, but didn't know it."

"I may never forgive you."

"You will, but not for a while – maybe. Now you know you're okay. Better get back. They may actually need us," said Jonesy.

"Damn I hate when you're right," Dee said. She started to get up.

Jonesy gestured for her to stay. "There's probably going to be some drinking on this boat. You should stay to see that it – the drinking at least – doesn't get out of hand."

"Are you suborning fraternization?"

"No, ma'am. That would make me an accomplice to intimate relations engaged in between an active duty officer and an active duty enlisted – among other things. Did I get that right chief?"

"Close enough, Jonesy. Close enough."

"Then, there's no way," said Dee as she continued to rise.

"Let me introduce," said Jonesy, "Maritime Law Enforcement Specialist Chief Scott Jackson – United States Coast Guard – retired."

Dee stopped halfway to her feet. "Retired?"

"Yup. Two days ago. Quick retirement was a favor from a friend. No longer subject to the UCMJ."

Heading up the ladder, Jonesy said, over her shoulder, "He'll get you back safe and sound, lieutenant. Probably not today. Don't worry, we'll cover."

There was a bump and then the sound of the response boat heading away.

"So, I've been Shanghaied?"

"Well, not Shanghaied. More of a sleepover. I've got a few things in the bedroom if you want to change out of those," he said indicating her uniform.

"Maybe I like being in my uniform."

"Well, I like you whether you are in or out of your uniform."

Dee blushed. "That's not fair. We shouldn't have –"

"But we did. And even if it meant the end of my career, I am glad we did. I just didn't want it to be a problem for you. You've got your whole career ahead of you. I didn't want to end it – especially in dishonor."

"Leave it to the military and Coast Guard to equate love with dishonor," she said. "I've thought about that night a lot.

"Yeah. Me too. Why don't you change and I'll pour some champagne?"

She emerged a few minutes later wearing an electric blue bikini. "So, who was the previous owner of these?"

"Holy cow," he said when he saw her.

"Answer the question."

"Jonesy got your sizes. No previous owner, but Jesus, don't let the enlisted see you in that. They'll be falling off the boats and piers."

"It would serve you right," she said, taking a glass of champagne. "You're going to have to start cutting back, though. You can't afford a yacht or a rich lifestyle on your retired pay."

"Don't have to. My family has a business. Maritime security. I'm now an owner and VP. Not everyone makes the grade. You have to complete an honorable military career as a requirement. I'll do okay. The boat belongs to the family business."

"Anything else I should know?" she asked, sipping her champagne.

"I love you, Dee Cruise," he said

"I know."

"I want to tell you every day."

"You do. I love you too."

He kissed her softly. "You know, the first time you kissed me – in the donut shop – I felt like I'd experienced heaven."

"Just the first time?" she asked coyly.

"Every time. But the first time – the first time was worth waiting a lifetime. Whenever I look at you, I see your lips and remember how that kiss felt."

Scott dropped to his knees and kissed her stomach – heat and an electric current filled her immediately. "Now that you know my future is secure and we're not going to jail, I'm going to do everything I can to convince a certain lieutenant that she should take me as her husband. But, do I have to call you lieutenant?"

"Of course not, silly. I'll get promoted – and you can call me commander."

He sighed, then, "As you wish. You're going to get cold if that's all you're wearing. When the sun goes down, it really gets cold out here. I should get you forward and under a blanket. For warmth, you know."

"Yeah, you're forward alright. I suppose you'll want to get something warm into me."

"Why, lieutenant, you read my mind."

"You still have to ask permission to come aboard."

"Do I need to salute the captain?"

"I have an idea that's already happening."

He stood, kissed her, lifted her into his arms and carried her to the bedroom.

Fifty-three

Commander Dee Cruise watched from the bridge wing as the lines tying up the four-hundred-foot Legend class Coast Guard Cutter were doubled up and gangway was placed. It had been a four-day patrol, now there were some routine maintenance tasks that would take two weeks to complete. A shiny black Mercedes-Benz S Class sedan was parked in the lot beside the pier. A man wearing dress slacks and a Tori Richard Hawaiian print shirt was leaning against the driver side door.

A lieutenant walked up behind her. "All tied up and doubled up, Skipper. I'll give the order to go cold iron and set the watch on your okay."

"Very well. Give the orders."

"Aye, aye, ma'am. Your ride?" He gestured toward the car in the lot.

"Yes. My ride," she smiled. "You have my number if anything comes up. I'll want a report daily on the progress of work, issues, anything else that seems worthy."

"Yes, ma'am. Enjoy your leave. We'll take good care of her for you while you're gone."

Dee turned, crossed the bridge, descended the internal ladders and headed out onto the deck. The quarterdeck watch saluted smartly and greeted her.

"Captain."

She returned the salute, stepped onto the gang plank, and when she'd crossed over the side of the ship, saluted the flag on the stern. The ship's bell rang twice and over the ship's loudspeaker system came, "San Lorenzo, departing." The ship's bell rang once again.

She walked down the gang plank with as much dignity and military bearing as she could muster, and restrained herself from running to the waiting car.

Scott immediately put his arms around her and pulled her tight against him. His lips crushed hers.

"The crew will see what we're doing!" she said, but she didn't pull away.

"It's a good thing they can't see what I'm thinking."

She started to blush, and a warm cozy feeling started to spread inside her. "Well, it isn't proper while I'm in uniform," she said in a mock serious voice.

"Yeah? Well the first thing I'm going to do is get you out of uniform."

"That will be more than two hours from now – when we get to the resort."

"Not true," he whispered in her ear. "I found a nice little secluded spot not fifteen minutes from here. Grass. Trees. I've got a blanket."

"Scott!" She was bright red. "We couldn't. I couldn't. I mean, married people don't –" but the warm cozy feeling was betraying her – starting to burn more intensely.

"Uh huh. Tell me that when your legs start shaking." He walked her to the passenger side and opened her door. Before she got in, he kissed her again. He returned to the driver's side got in.

She took his hand in hers. "You know, my mother always warned me not to trust sailors. But I wouldn't have it any other way."

He started the car and music started playing from his phone.

"Wait! What's that song?" she asked.

"Are you kidding. It's Kelly Clarkson," but the rest of his response was lost as they roared down the pier.

About this Book

The United States Coast Guard was founded in 1790 and has a long proud history. More than one hundred coastguardsmen were killed in action during the 1944 D-Day invasion of Europe. Coastguardsmen have also served in action in other conflicts as well – riding small boats on the rivers of Viet Nam and riverine operations in Iraq, for example. During peacetime, the Coast Guard performs drug interdiction, stops human trafficking and provides security of our ports and shores against those wishing to do us harm – along with about a dozen other missions vital to our nation.

This is a book of fiction. Any similarity to any persons or events is coincidental. Fraternization between active duty personnel is a crime punishable under the Uniform Code of Military Justice (UCMJ), although fraternization does occur from time to time, despite those punishments. Love, in real life as in fiction, sometimes does conquer all. Similarly, crimes like those attributed to fictional Captain Trahir do occur – rarely – and are punished severely, as they should be. The vast majority of Coast Guard officers and enlisted personnel perform their duties with honor and distinction. When you see them, please thank them for their service. They go to war against a vast array of miscreants and enemies on a daily basis.

Anna Leigh

For those who may have a knowledge of the French language, trahir is the French verb for "to betray."

Thank you for reading my book. I hope you enjoyed it.

If you liked this book, <u>please leave a review on Amazon</u>. Reviews help other readers find books they would like to read and help authors improve their own works.

In addition, if you would like to be one of my beta reviewers – someone who reads my books before publication and who receives the completed book free of charge, please send your name and e-mail address to my publisher at <u>TWeaver2008@aol.com</u> to be included in this group. You may opt out at any time. You can also contact me through my website <u>https://www.annaleighromance.com/</u>

Books by Anna Leigh

<u>Loves Lost and Found</u> – A Mystery Romance Adventure

<u>Lost in the Forest</u> – A Romantic Wilderness Adventure

<u>River Cruise Undercover</u> – A Romantic Travel Adventure

<u>Rocky Mountain Romance</u>

<u>Shallow Water Romance</u> – A Story of Forbidden Love and Adventure

ABOUT THE AUTHOR

Anna Leigh lives in suburban Maryland. She enjoys musical theater, loves to travel, and cares for small animals. She also enjoys fitness activities, has completed numerous Spartan challenges, and placed in her class in the Strongest Woman Maryland competition.

Made in the USA
Columbia, SC
24 March 2020